Inklings Book 2017

The following young authors contributed their short stories and poems to this anthology.

Andrew Chu	Oliver Jackson	Amanvir Parhar
Camille Chu	Dylan Lefever	Louisa Pflaum
Lauren Crawford	Jude Lewis	Lily Shi
Saketh Elumalai	Claire Lignore	Samuel Teoh
Elena García	Shannon Ma	Lila Tierney
Tiffanie Huang	Zachary Marinov	Claire Wong
Toby Jacob	Lauren Meier	Ann Yang

Thank you to the following mentors for contributing editorial guidance and letters.

Philomena Block	Kim Culbertson	Loraine McCormick
Jena Brigantino	Malar Ganapathiappan	Briana Mitchell
Jenn Castro	Naomi Kinsman	Erica Morgan
Ernesto Cisneros	Madeline Knutson	Sarah Lyn Rogers
Ailynn Knox-Collins	Polly McCann	Kristi Wright

Cover illustration by Lea Lyon (*www.lealyon.com*)
Copyedited by Sarah Lyn Rogers
Edited by Naomi Kinsman

Printed in the USA
First Printing: August 2017
ISBN: 978-0-9981849-1-3

Contents

Thank you to our Patrons!

Andrew Avallone	Christine Dowd	Rick Schermerhorn
Karen Bechtel	Odette Harris	Laura Schmidt
Rebecca Behrens	Marilyn Hilton	Oriana Siska
Joanna Bradshaw	Ann Jacobus	Zufishan Shah
David Butler	Patricia Newman	Kelly Smith
Bear Capron	Sue Penchina	Raina Telgemeier
Kamryn Clarke	Sarah Perez	Ashley Walker
Jill Davis	Tracy Piombo	Patrick York
Mandy Davis	Helen Pyne	Anne Young

Foreword

At Society of Young Inklings, we love connecting young writers with grown-up authors. Something magical happens when children are able to share their work and discuss it seriously with an adult who's been there before. The *Inklings Book 2017* is our ninth annual anthology featuring stories and poems by writers in grades one through eight. This anthology includes stories and poems featuring talking fruits, dramatic legislative rulings, the grim reaper, fairies, and anthropomorphized germs, to name just some of the varied subjects young writers brought to us this year.

Selecting the winning submissions is a challenge every year, as the quality and quantity of submissions is always impressive. After much deliberation, our editorial team chose twenty-one pieces to publish this year. All of the winners were chosen for their commendable writing skills, but winning is just the beginning! Each winner then worked with a Society of Young Inklings mentor to clarify any places where the writer's creative vision was unclear and showcase the writer's natural strengths in their work.

A "Dear Reader" letter accompanies each story and poem in this book. Written by the mentors, these letters explain the revision process each young writer went through and provide guidance on how to use these tools in your own writing. We hope the wonderful stories and poems in this book–along with the stories of how they changed through revision–will touch you, entertain you, and encourage you to dive into your own writing projects!

If you're feeling inspired by this anthology and looking for more ways to be part of the Inklings community, be sure to check out our mentorship opportunities, classes, writing prompts, and other offerings at *www.younginklings.org*.

Creating Mood

Jenn Castro advised Elena García on using sensory details to create a mood of homesickness in Elena's story, "Luciérnagas."

Dear Reader,

Creating mood in a story is important. How does the writer know when she has enough dialogue and description so the reader feels he or she is a part of the story? Elena García's "Luciérnagas" impressed our team of readers right away because of Elena's ability to capture the mood of the story. When Elena and I met to revise her story, there wasn't anything that needed fixing in the story. However, we wondered if because Elena was so skilled at creating mood, she might be able to use this ability to create even stronger atmosphere in her story.

We brainstormed the places where Elena had developed feeling, and then she dreamed up one or two additional places in her story where mood could be enhanced even more. One of those spots was in the end, just before Julia remembers the fireflies. Elena wanted to include words in her story to make the reader feel Julia's initial homesickness in her new house. Using the five senses, we listed things a child might miss from her old life. The other was when the mom and dad reveal to Julia that the family is moving to the United States of America. Here we talked about gradually elevating the anger Julia felt about her parents' decision to move. At first, Elena thought she might make many changes to her story, but in the end her revision included only two simple changes.

Elena did some important work that all writers must do in revision. First, she brainstormed more ideas than she might need in her story. Second, she considered all the moments in her story she could change. Then Elena had to make choices. Sometimes, when we start looking at revising a story, we see place after place that we could change. The key to revision, especially when a writer is near the end of the writing process, is to be careful about not making so many changes that the story becomes bloated with new ideas. Elena's skill was in carefully choosing where to add new dialogue or thoughts of her character. I was impressed with the way Elena knew immediately which parts of her story needed a few more enhancers.

If you're writing a story, you might try Elena's revision approach. Read over your story with someone else, and look for places you could change. Think of ways you can build on what you've already written well. Next, brainstorm at least five ways you might use any of the five senses to create more mood in your story. Before making final changes, look again at your story to make sure the changes are needed and make your story's mood even stronger. Read the story not as a writer, but as a reader. Do your new ideas fit? Do they enhance the mood in your story? You will know because you will feel what you want your reader to feel! Remember, like Elena, you may only change one or two phrases or sentences or pieces of dialogue, but you might find that these small additions will make your story even stronger and more of what you wanted it to be.

Like Elena advises, have fun revising!

Jenn Castro

Jenn Castro is the author of *Mom Me*, a children's picture book about a kid who only wants to play with Mom. Jenn has always written—on napkins, backs of envelopes, and in newspapers, diaries, and journals. Jenn loves any kind of children's book, especially coming-of-age stories and middle grade chapter books about ordinary young people. In addition to children's books, Jenn also writes about parenting, stop signs, and other quirky parts of life as a guest blogger and on her website, *jenncastro.com*. A Young Inklings mentor and teacher, Jenn lives in California with her husband and two kids.

Elena García

Elena is in fourth grade at Nixon Elementary in Palo Alto, California. She plays soccer and likes to read and write. She loves a good mystery and wants to be a writer with cliffhangers that have no end. Her favorite animal is the dog because it symbolizes loyalty and playfulness. Elena read *The Phantom Tollbooth* when she was six and ever since, it has been impossible for her to put a good book down.

Jenn Castro: What revision techniques did you use to add more mood to the dialogue at the end of your story?
Elena García: In my last paragraph, I pictured Julia's feelings. I tried to imagine how she was feeling moving into a new house in a new country. I knew that section needed one or two more sentences to make sure the reader could sense Julia was worried about her new place.

Q: What advice do you have for Inklings who are revising?
A: Be open to what others tell you. Think about what the character feels and what you want the reader to feel.

Q: When did you start writing?
A: I started writing in first or second grade.

Q: Where do you like to write?

A: I write at school and at home. When I'm at school, I write on a bench outside. It's peaceful. I don't like lots of noise when I'm writing. At home, I write in my room or on the couch where it's comfortable.

Q: What do you like about writing?

A: I enjoy making up stories that take the reader away.

Q: How do you come up with your ideas?

A: I think about what's going on with me in my world. Then I try to put some of what I'm feeling in my character. When I read books, I can feel characters' emotions. I can see landscapes. I want my readers to feel and see what my characters are feeling and seeing.

Q: Do you ever feel blocked? What do you do?

A: I get a glass of water. I get some exercise to clear my mind. I think, "Okay, how am I going to do this?"

Luciérnagas

by
Elena García

Fireflies danced in the night sky of Mexico, lighting the darkness. I sighed, watching them fly up and down. They were beautiful.

"Aren't they wonderful, Mamá?"

Mamá turned around from cooking her homemade *fideo seco*, my favorite food.

"Sí, they are, Julia!" she said, smiling.

I returned the smile and looked out again, but the fireflies had disappeared. I sighed and lifted myself off the wooden chair and went to help Mamá. The fideo seco smelled so good that I wanted to grab it out of the pan! But I knew better and started to get the table ready. Once everything was ready, I sat down on a chair and licked my lips.

"Eh, eh, eh," Mamá said, washing her hands. "Go tell Papá that dinner is ready."

I ran as fast as I could to my parents' room. Papá was typing on the computer.

Panting, I said, "Papá . . . dinner is ready . . . and it's fideo seco!"

"Sí, sí, sí. I'm coming."

He laughed and got up. I kept pushing him out the door. He was walking very slowly, although he is usually the fastest one here. After centuries he finally sat down on his wooden chair and dinner began. I started to gobble up the food, flavors bursting in my mouth every second! But Mamá gave me a stern look, which I knew meant, *Manners*!

I quickly replaced my gobbling with little bites.

As we ate, my parents talked about grownup problems, while I thought about the fireflies I had seen by the window and many more things.

I thought about Sophia and Alejandro, my two best amigos. I thought about the poems I made and the stories I had read. I thought about numbers and letters that confused me, all the while eating the most delicious food on Earth. Since I was thinking so deep about my life, I almost didn't hear my parents call my name.

"Julia!"

"Huh?" I said, looking back and forth between them.

Mamá sighed. "Julia, your Papá and I were talking, and um, you might not go to La Escuela Fina De Niñas anymore."

It took a moment to take in what Mom had just said.

"*What*?!"

Mamá sighed sadly. "I know, I know."

I was raging. La Escuela Fina De Niñas was the best school ever! All of my friends went there!

"Why can't I go to school anymore?" My voice was growing louder.

Papá and Mamá looked at each other, then at me.

Papá took a deep breath, looked at me real serious, and said three words: "We are moving."

My mouth hung low in an oval. What had he just said? We might be moving!? My mind was racing in circles. I thought I was going to throw up. The fideo seco in my mouth tasted foul. I pushed it away.

"Where are we moving to?" I said.

Papá and Mamá looked at each other for a second, then at me.

"The United States of America."

"The what?"

"The United States of America."

"Huh?"

My mom sighed with exasperation. "It is the country right above Mexico."

I stared at her in pure confusion. "There is a country in the sky?"

Papá laughed. Mamá stifled a little giggle, too. I looked at Papá and Mamá, pitying them. Poor souls, they think there is a country in the sky. I shook my head. Parents these days.

Papá and Mamá were still laughing and I was getting annoyed.

"What!!" I shouted. I could feel my ears turning pink.

Papá and Mamá stopped laughing. Mamá nudged Papá to keep talking. He looked confused. Mamá gave him a look that said, *Explain*. Papá cleared his throat and said, "Julia, the United States of America is not in the sky. It is one of Mexico's neighboring countries and is to the north."

"Oh," I said.

I started to laugh, thinking how dumb I was. A country in the

sky! What was I thinking! What comes next? Flying pigs? My parents started laughing with me. We all laughed our hearts out, thinking about the country in the sky.

∽ ●◆ ∽

It was August, three months after the announcement that we were moving. It was drastically true. I looked out the car window as the car descended into the great city of San Francisco. I looked at the manual for getting to know San Fran. ("That is what the hipsters call it," Papá had said earlier.) I flipped through the pages of the manual and finally found the Spanish section. I saw a page that caught my eye.

THE GOLDEN GATE BRIDGE

There was a picture of the bridge below the title. I looked it over and over. I was confused. The bridge was red! I tapped Mamá on the shoulder. "Mamá, why is the bridge red? It says 'Golden Gate Bridge.'"

Mamá looked at me over from the rearview mirror and laughed.

"Ay, ay, ay! My *hija*, the bridge is actually named for the Golden Gate Strait."

"*Qué*? What?"

Papá, still looking on the road ahead, said, "Julia, the Golden Gate Strait is the narrow entrance between the Pacific Ocean and the San Francisco Bay."

"Why is the strait golden?"

Mamá sighed. "Oh, Julia."

Papá chuckled.

We stopped in front of a red house. It was small, but just the right size for a family of three. We hauled the luggage to the front porch.

Papá sighed. "Are you ready for a new adventure?"

Mamá and I looked at each other.

"We're ready."

Papá opened the door. It was a quaint house, with two stories, and a little kitchen. It was growing dark, so Mamá told me to go to bed. As I ascended the stairs, it was already 8:30. Man. Bedtime. I plummeted onto the bed and sighed. I missed my friends already. It didn't help that the small room resembled nothing to my previous one. Even the smell in the air was unfamiliar, stuffy and damp. This was all much different from my old home. My parents came and gave me a good night's kiss. Then I was all alone. I felt hollow. Suddenly, something came to me.

"Please, please, please," I whispered.

I pulled the curtains apart from the window, revealing the night sky. I looked. Nothing. I looked harder, and then I saw them. There were many. Twinkling lights in the darkness. They flew through the air, darting back and forth, making me laugh. As I watched them, I knew that even though it would be hard, in the end, everything would be all right.

Humor through Surprise

Philomena Block mentored Jude Lewis through a revision focused on using specific details to create humorous surprises in his story, "The Mixed-Up Tale."

Dear Reader,

Humor through surprise can be very serious business. How do you make a story funnier while still keeping the plot moving forward and interesting? Jude Lewis's story, "The Mixed-Up Tale," stood out to our team of readers because of Jude's strong sense of humor and creativity. When Jude and I met to revise his story, I applauded that Jude had awesome ideas and a great sense of humor. However, I knew we could take it to the next level. I knew that with a few more tools, he could turn his funny tale into a sidesplitting story.

We started with a statement that I learned when studying comedy writing: "Never say 'candy bar' when you can say 'Milky Way.'" In comedy, the more specific you can be, the funnier your statement. Which is funnier: "hat" or "purple striped zebra beanie with giant pom-poms"? The more details you include, the more opportunities for humor. People respond to specifics because they are more real and relatable than vague details. We thought about how we could add details to Jude's story and make those details as specific as possible. Jude added specifics and sensory details as a great way to add humor and surprise the reader. Jude also included lots of "asides" in his story. We used asides to refer to statements that we wrote in parentheses to add commentary to the humor. Jude's original draft had a few of these asides and I encouraged him to take his commentary to the next level and add more of them. You'll see his final version on the next pages.

Jude did a few very important things that all writers must do in his revision. First, he gave himself the chance to make his ideas big, bigger, and the biggest they could be. Sometimes, we are afraid to expand our imaginations even when we are writing fiction. We are worried others won't understand our jokes and that stops us from taking risks. The problem with this approach, however, is that we limit ourselves. Sometimes the idea we most need is there but we are too afraid to write it down.

The second important thing Jude did was to add commentary. Sometimes we worry about "breaking the narrative." Even in a funny story, we might be afraid to take a writing risk like commentary and asides. This approach can make our writing too serious and boring. I was impressed with the way Jude made his story more surprising, interesting, and hilarious with these approaches.

If you're writing a funny story, you might try Jude's revision approach. Read over your story and find parts that could be more specific. Then, make your ideas more specific and as big as they can be. Next, look back at your story and add more details and commentary. Do any of these ideas make you giggle or smile? Make choices about what to include and what to leave out. Remember, you may change more than you expected, or find yourself writing about crazy surprising details, but you might find that these changes make your story better.

Happy writing,
Philomena Block

Philomena Block is an actress, educator, and comedian from Santa Cruz, California. Philomena holds two bachelor's degrees—one in musical theatre, the other in psychology—and is trained in playwriting, sketch comedy, and improvisation. She has been inspiring young writers with Society of Young Inklings for the last two years, and is thrilled to mentor for the first time this year! Philomena has always been drawn to storytelling and considers herself an avid "comedy nerd." When Philomena isn't teaching or performing, you can catch her baking or enjoying the great outdoors.

Jude Lewis

Jude is a second grader at Duniway School in Portland, Oregon. He plays soccer and baseball but spends most of his time reading. When he grows up, he wants to be an author and travel the world. He has already lived on three continents, traveled to ten countries, and visited fifteen states in the USA—but there is still so much more to explore. His favorite not-mixed-up fairy tale is "Jack and the Beanstalk"!

Philomena Block: How did you come up with your idea for "The Mixed-Up Tale"?

Jude Lewis: I was doing a unit on fairy tales at school. We were reading the fairy tales and looked at what features they had in them. There were good people and there were bad people. I wanted to make my own version of them.

Q: What are your favorite books?

A: I really really like the Harry Potter series. I like the magic and the adventure of Harry Potter. I also really like Percy Jackson, because I like the Greek gods and I like to learn about them (Greek gods) on my own. I also loved *Escape from Mr. Lemoncello's Library*, because it's in a library. I like books and it mentions lots of books, and I like games and there are a lot of board and card games.

Q: What changed when you revised to add humor from surprise?

A: Well . . . it got funnier. I liked it better with the new parts in it.

Q: What was your favorite new part you added during your revision?

A: The aside about the last time the wolf ate something sweet. I thought the end of that was really funny.

Q: What advice do you have for other Inklings who don't like revision very much?

A: It was pretty fun thinking of new ideas. I was nervous. If you are going to try and revise your story to be more comedic, when changing language, Philomena taught me to be specific and "Never say 'candy bar' when you can say 'Milky Way.'" That was helpful.

The Mixed-Up Tale

by

Jude Lewis

Once upon a time, there was an old gray wolf. The wolf lived with three lazy pigs. The pigs slept in the wolf's barn and had to clean up all the horse manure. The wolf was extremely frustrated with the pigs because they weren't doing anything. The manure was piling up and really stinky and the wolf had had enough! So, one day, he sold the three pigs to Milky White, the cow, for some magic eggs. (You might expect beans, but you see, magic beans weren't invented at the time.)

He got home and ate the magic eggs for supper. Crack, slurp, crack, slurp. He was so hungry he gobbled them down with the shells on. (I don't know if you've ever tasted magic eggs, but they taste like prune juice on grandmas. You might think that sounds disgusting, but since grandmas are his favorite food, the wolf loved it!)

"Nothing will happen to me!" he said.

When he woke up, there was an eggstalk in his bed and he was on the floor.

"Hmmm! What's going on?" exclaimed the wolf. Now, this wolf knew a lot about fairy tales. He knew that a giant lived up that eggstalk and he also knew that the giant had a pot of gold up there. But he didn't want to climb up it. (If you actually experience one, you will think it is very slimy.)

So, instead of going up the eggstalk, he shouted, "Get down or I'll huff and puff and blow it all down."

The giant bellowed, "No! I'm waiting for a boy called Jack." (You would feel angry and annoyed if someone was always shouting at you!)

So the wolf huffed and puffed and tried to blow the eggstalk down. But he only succeeded in blowing the giant off the eggstalk. (If you try to break one you will see it is very strong.) So the giant went to the hospital. Fortunately, he only broke his pinky finger! (Now you know there is no such thing as giant hospital so he had to poke his pinky finger through the window of a regular hospital and it took all the bandages in the hospital to fix. The doctors and nurses felt super surprised when a giant turned up!)

The next day he was back up the eggstalk and the wolf shouted, "Come down or I'll climb up and eat your grandma!"

The giant said, "I'm fighting Jack right now. Come back tomorrow! Plus my grandma isn't alive anymore!"

When he heard this, the wolf felt very sad. (I know what you're thinking. You're thinking that the wolf feels sad for the giant because he lost his grandma but he's actually disappointed because, as you know, grandmas are his favorite food and he didn't get to eat her!)

So, that night, the wolf climbed up the slimy eggstalk because the giant refused to come down. He brought out an old, rusty sword that he had from the Big War of the Bridge with the Troll Under It and a big blue backpack (the kind that's good for carrying heavy things in). When he got up the eggstalk, he found two enormous guard chickens. They were wearing red crash helmets and guarding a crooked wooden gate. The wolf stood in front of the chickens, sweating and shaking. The chickens were clucking, flapping their wings, and kicking skulls at the wolf. He swung his sword and chopped the talons off one of their feet. The chicken bit back on the end of the wolf's nose. The wolf screamed like an elephant blowing his trunk and ran away. It was pretty hard to defeat them. (It seemed like they were invincible!) Suddenly he had a brilliant idea. He called his friend the Pied Piper, who played a little melody that sent them right to sleep. (No, silly! The wolf didn't have a phone. He called by shouting down the eggstalk. Luckily, the Pied Piper was catching frogs nearby!) The wolf silently tiptoed past the chickens and through the gate.

Next, the wolf traveled through a deep, dark forest, until he found a gigantic house made of candy. Unfortunately, he couldn't eat or touch the candy because he was allergic to anything sweet and if he did his head would swell like a balloon. (Let me tell you about the last time the wolf ate something sweet. He was just minding his own business, going for a walk, but he got lost. The wolf found a little cottage and knocked on the door. An old woman and an old man opened the door. They offered him a gingerbread man but it ran out the door, shouting, "Run, run as fast as you can, you'll never catch up with the gingerbread man!" The wolf wanted that gingerbread man so badly. [He didn't know then that he was allergic to sweet things.] He chased after the gingerbread man until they came to a river. The gingerbread man couldn't figure out how to get across, so the wolf

jumped at the gingerbread man and tore his head off! He took a bite and immediately his head swelled up like a balloon. The wolf's head weighed him down so much he fell into the river and floated away. Now you see why the wolf does not eat or touch anything sweet!)

He grabbed some pliers from his backpack and twisted the doorknob (which was a red gumdrop—just looking at it made him feel queasy). He slipped inside. Luckily for him, the floor was made of wood! He found himself in a messy kitchen and had to sneak past the pots and pans without making any noise. The wolf had a look at the clock and realized it was ten o'clock at night. He headed for the pantry because he was starting to get hungry. He stole some bread from the pantry. (He had to pick out all the little kid bones.) After a while, he fell into a deep sleep.

In the morning the giant sniffed suspiciously around and boomed, "Fe fi fo fum, I smell some wolf bones to put in my rum."

The wolf hid (but not in a good spot). The giant sneaked up behind him, grabbed him, shoved him in a cage, and locked it with a key.

Meanwhile, the three pigs had escaped Milky White and were in the wolf's house. They found the eggstalk but not him so they climbed up it. They found the giant's house and the wolf in a cage getting ready to be cooked.

"Why did you come back?" asked the wolf, feeling surprised that they would come back after he had sold them.

The first one said, "We wanted to know where you were."

The second added, "We had to escape that cow."

"Plus, he was going to eat us," the third one chimed in.

The giant was just walking by when the first pig grabbed the key from the giant's pocket. They shoved it in the lock and turned it. Then they quickly jabbed it back into his pocket (too quickly for the giant to notice it). The wolf jumped out of the cage and took a deep breath. They all bounded off the counter, as quickly as someone who has accidently sat on hedgehog, and sped out of the door.

Suddenly, a group of witches came out of nowhere. The short one with the very pointed nose started to cackle and said, "I can cackle better than any of you."

Another one with brown crooked teeth said, "No, I'm the best cackler!"

Then they all started to argue about who was the best at cackling until the witch with lots of warts yelled, "Stop it! We're supposed to be destroying these little brats!"

Everyone immediately snapped out of it. The witches crowded around the pigs and the wolf. The pigs' teeth were chattering and little oinks could be heard from them. The wolf's fur was standing up on end. Just then there was a rustle in the bushes and suddenly out popped an old lady in a torn dress. Using her fists, she knocked the witches out one by one. (The wolf sort of wanted to eat her because she smelled a lot like a grandma but she had just saved their lives so he decided not to. You know how tough that must have been for him. The wolf *loved* grandmas [eating them, not hugging them!]). The wolf and the pigs just stared with their mouths open.

"What are you waiting for? Get down that eggstalk!" shouted the old lady.

The wolf, the pigs, and the old lady rushed down the eggstalk just to find the witches in the living room of the wolf's house (witches are magical, you know that!). All at once, something flew out from

behind the couch. That something surprisingly was Cinderella.

"Ugh. I've been hunting those witches for months." And with one flick of her wrist she bopped the witches on the head with her glass slipper, and they got knocked out. Cinderella went off to hunt her next criminal, which turned out to be Red Riding Hood (that mean wolf-slaying little girl!). The old woman ran off because she was nearly late for her karate class. The wolf and the pigs became friends and lived together. They all lived happily ever. Except for the witches because now they had to clean out manure in the wolf's barn.

(Maybe you're wondering what happened to the giant? Let me tell you. Later that day, the mailman arrived to deliver a brand new shovel for the witches [lucky them!] and drove his truck straight into the eggstalk. It fell down, splashed into the river, and floated away. Now the giant was stuck. And if you listen very carefully you can still hear him bellowing in anger today.)

The Promise of the Story

Malar Ganapathiappan guided Andrew Chu through a revision to emphasize the promise of his story, "The Tie Breaker."

Dear Reader,

I was impressed by Andrew's story, "The Tie Breaker." It has a fascinating, relevant premise with realistic characters. Historical and political events, family and identity issues, major decision-making . . . wow! Layering so many significant pieces can be especially tricky to do in a short story. Andrew did this with a wonderfully strong command of language.

For the revision focus, I asked Andrew to identify the promise of his story. Was it related to Julia's past or her present decision? Balancing this in both the beginning and end gives the reader a sense of completion.

The first chapter set the tone and drew the reader into Julia's past. Contrastingly, Andrew's original ending seemed abrupt, leaving more questions than answers. Conclusions don't have to provide all the answers, but satisfying ones answer most of the reader's crucial questions. Answering or closing enough questions will leave your reader fulfilled instead of confused or discontented. You control what ideas the reader ends with. After more of the story's loose ends were tied up and the major focus was returned to, the reader gained a stronger sense of completion and clarity of the story's promise.

We also discussed ways to play around with details in order to highlight the main points and overarching values. The final edits are meant to fine-tune a story. Andrew tweaked his paragraphs and sentences with care for portraying what he wanted to get across to his reader. The results are masterful!

Malar Ganapathiappan

Malar Ganapathiappan finds joy in stories and loves sharing inspiration and creativity with others. She earned a psychology BA summa cum laude. While not reading, writing, or instructing, she enjoys exploring the outdoors.

Andrew Chu

Andrew is a seventh grader at The Nueva School. He is an avid reader, and also enjoys playing sports and music. Andrew also enjoys following the current events and politics of the world. His story, "The Tie Breaker," integrated Andrew's love for writing and politics, and was inspired by the beliefs of a certain US politician. The story was originally intended to be a fictional novella. However, with an unpredicted turn of events in the 2016 elections, the story has slowly started to become a more realistic novella.

Malar Ganapathiappan: How did you get the idea for your story and to combine these particular ideas?

Andrew Chu: It all originally started when my family visited Alcatraz and I learned about a very old escape from Alcatraz. This story was inspired by the 2016 political climate. It was written before the 2016 elections. I originally wrote it as a fictional novella to model a very rare possibility of what the future could look like. After the election happened, the story evolved to a more realistic novella.

Q: How did you decide on your characters?

A: I thought less explicitly of what my characters would be. It was more of what kind of personalities and traits of a character would fit the plot the best. I didn't have the characters in mind at first but as the plot changed, the characters evolved also.

Q: How long did it take you to write this story? What was your writing process?

A: It took two to two and a half months to finish the story. The first draft took two weeks to complete. I wrote in pieces and had at least over twenty drafts. The plot evolved on its own as I learned about the Alcatraz escape. It started with being about Alcatraz. Then I integrated what I'd learned in Spanish class about immigration in Texas with US/Mexico borders, and then politics. It kind of wrote itself. The plot changed every time I tried to edit it.

Q: How do you feel about the changes you made?

A: I made changes mainly to improve the clarity of story. Some changes have been to make it more easy to understand. They were minor partly because I originally wrote the story just for friends and not a big audience. To a reader who hasn't gone through the same process of research and writing I've gone through, I think the added information makes a difference.

Q: Why do you enjoy writing?

A: I love reading and debate. Writing is a place in the middle. It's a great way to express opinions and convey emotions which you can't really do with anything else. It's a way to explain yourself in a more explicit way. You can tell a lot about a writer through their writing without knowing anything about them explicitly. It's a great way to express myself. It's interesting to enjoy reading and then write on my own.

The Tie Breaker

by

Andrew Chu

Author's Note: I started writing this fictional novella in September 2016 as a simple farce, inspired by my family's summer visit to Alcatraz. However, the surprising turn of political events from the Fall of 2016 has turned it into realistic fiction. I hope you enjoy it and that it continues to predict future political developments!

Chapter One

Before the letters came, Julia Morgan had always thought the most important day of her life was the day two years ago when the President of the United States had called her. From growing up with her mother in an all-but-forgotten city in Texas to being appointed a justice on the Supreme Court by the President, Julia knew she had come a long way. She had assumed her life had taken all its major turns. But that was all before the letters came.

Julia had spent her childhood in Laredo, Texas, a border city

just a river away from Mexico. Laredo was known for its outrageous festivals, including Border Beer Fest and Jalapeño Day. Remarkably, it had a sister city, Nuevo Laredo, in another country but only a few miles away! Nuevo Laredo was part of the Mexican state of Tamaulipas which itself had an impressive history. Humans had lived there for over 8,000 years and Tamaulipas had been the home of one of Mexico's first ports. Because of the proximity of the two cities, there was more exposure to the different cultures than typical for sister cities. Many citizens spoke both languages, one fluidly and the other sufficiently fragmented. However, a single river also carved vast differences. Although the Rio Grande was only two hundred feet wide at some points, its powerful current frightened immigrants from crossing. Close relatives, sometimes even immediate family, lived on opposite sides of the Rio Grande. Because strict laws and complex visiting processes made it hard to actually visit the other, relatives would occasionally wave to each other across the narrowest parts of the river. These semi-reunions would leave Julia standing awkwardly by her mother's side, blushing at her lack of Mexican family and occasionally waving to the relatives of her best friend, Alejandra, instead.

Not only did Julia not have a Mexican family to wave to, she also lacked any visible Mexican heritage. She had a distinct European look that stood out in her community. Her Mexicano neighbors had skins of beautifully blended shades. As a young girl, Julia always felt her skin was too pale and her face too angular. She knew she was just being self-conscious as Alejandra and the other children treated her as one of their own. They giggled together while running around playing children's games such as Escondidas and La Gallinita Ciega on the dusty side streets. And Julia's mother had always told her to accept herself and, more importantly, to accept others. *Welcome people, Julia Cherise, even if they aren't part of your community*.

Julia knew this was an important message because her mother only used her middle name on such occasions. So this is what Julia did. Although, as she grew older, it occurred to her that her mother, who would never tell Julia a thing about her father, was being hypocritical. How accepting was it to not tell Julia even her father's first or last name? When Julia asked, her mother would either ignore the question or dismiss it as if she had answered it a thousand times before. He remained a complete mystery and, eventually, Julia stopped asking.

Julia's mother worked two jobs to support the two of them. One was as a cashier at a fluorescently lit supermarket which made everyone, even the many Hispanic customers, look green. The other was at the Laredo public library where she shelved books. It was her mother's second job that fueled Julia's self-education. Her mother would leave her in the children's reading room with a pile of books on her right. By the time she came back from her shift, the pile would be on the left. Her mother assumed Julia had just been playing with the books, but actually, Julia always read the entire pile of books, cover to cover. Alejandra would sometimes join her. While her friend gravitated towards fiction books such as *Charlotte's Web* and, later, *Interview with the Vampire*, Julia found stories about talking pigs and monsters to be preposterous. She felt the world had enough problems to address without making up new, unbelievable ones. She loved books about the world such as *Laredo and Nuevo Laredo: A History across Countries*, as well as books about the law. Atticus Finch

was her hero.

Throughout Julia's life, immigration was one of the most-discussed topics in her community. Laredo had a respectable mayor and city hall—nothing to brag about, but not as shabby as other Texan cities. Laredo politicians were mostly Hispanic Americans who tended to agree with Laredo's citizens. But it was the federal government—the white politicians in DC—who were the focus of the hatred from Laredo citizens. Those white politicians' open but ignorant slander of Chicano immigrants was horrendous: Criminals! Rapists! Drug lords! Although Julia despised the name-calling, she was even more disappointed by the violent way the people of Nuevo Laredo expressed their opinions. When US border patrol boats were spotted, Mexicans of all ages would pick up rocks, and hurl them at the patrol boats.

This violence had a lasting effect on Julia. Alejandra's father had worked for the Coast Guard and one horrid afternoon he was pummeled by a rock thrown so viciously that it blinded him in one eye. Julia remembered her best friend sobbing hysterically when her father came home that night, wearing a pirate-like eye patch over his left eye along with a sad and defeated expression on his face. After this, Julia could not support Open Borders, even though she was a strong supporter of unity and peace across the border. If they threw rocks at the US authorities, she thought, imagine what they might do to US civilians.

When Julia grew up, she moved out of Texas, eager to reshape the politics of Washington, DC. She spent her college life studying foreign relations at Harvard, and eventually came to work in DC under the Bush administration. She was busy weaving her way through the intricate mazes of Washington politics when she received the news that her mother had passed away. She had immediately flown back to Laredo for a simple burial. Laredo now seemed so backwards and slow compared to the nation's capital. Julia realized there was nothing left for her in Laredo without her mother. Alejandra had long since moved away. Even her beloved children's reading room had been replaced by a Starbucks. The emptiness of the town forced Julia to jump on the first flight back to DC after the service. Remembering how hard her mother had worked for them, Julia threw herself into her own work like never before. She quickly rose to the US Second Court of Appeals. While her rulings were fair, her sentences showed her faith in humanity. When imprisonment was necessary, she always preferred shorter terms followed by rehabilitation.

During her decade-long tenure at the Court, she became known for her vote of For in the infamous case of *Doe ex. rel. Tarlow v. District of Columbia* and her vote of Against in *Colorado River Indian Tribes v. National Indian Gaming Commission*. These two rulings helped establish her reputation as being a fair but slightly conservative judge. She was proud of this reputation.

When the new President of the United States had been inaugurated, Julia did not think twice about the possibility of the Supreme Court. However, only a few months later, the esteemed Judge Conrad Carroll had unfortunately been diagnosed with prostate cancer and quickly stepped down. With the vacant seat, the rumors began to fly and Julia all but held her breath.

And so when the President called and asked her if she would accept the nomination, she of course said Yes. For a moment she wondered if it was poor form for a future Supreme Court judge to

start sobbing on the phone with the President, but she continued to cry with pride and joy anyhow. There was nothing she wanted more than to step onto the Supreme Court. She could help America in so many ways, from closing gun loopholes to reforming immigration. It was a big leap for a girl from a small town to rise to the highest court.

The first two years on the Court had been challenging. She had found herself to be the deciding vote in more than one case, tipping towards the four more conservative judges in the cases of *Jameson v. Board of Education* and *Ports v. Department of Health*. The President agreed with her rulings. She knew he was very pleased with her appointment.

However, this was all before the real event that transformed Julia's life—the letters.

Chapter Two

The day the first letter came, Julia had just returned home from another exhausting day in the Supreme Court. Six months of vicious arguments about the most recent case, *Larson v. The President*, were reaching a culmination, with a final decision only a week away. It was by far the most interesting case Julia had ever heard. It addressed the president's plan to build a physical barrier between the US and Mexico. This would add to Bush's 2006 Secure Fence Act. Somehow, even the 300 miles of vehicle fencing, 353 miles of pedestrian fencing, and video and aircraft surveillance had not been sufficient. Now the president thought a wall would be the solution, the only solution. But Gregory Larson, a liberal billionaire who thought the plan was ludicrous, had had the chutzpah to sue the president. In one of Larson's most famous speeches in Ann Arbor, he had galvanized the public by pointing out that the government's most conservative estimate of the cost just to build the wall was 25 billion dollars.

Despite Larson's zealous speeches, Julia suspected she would be the deciding vote. Four conservatives. Four liberals. And her. That was the unfortunate composition of the Supreme Court. The president obviously wanted her to lean conservatively and support his wall. As an "unbiased" judge, this is exactly what he had hired her to do. But she also thought of her Laredo friends waving to their Nuevo Laredo relatives across the river. A wall would change all this. However, although she also knew that the president could not technically kick her off the Supreme Court, he could probably make life very difficult for her if she disagreed with him.

This is what Julia was pondering as she walked into her posh, government-sponsored house in the upscale DC neighborhood of Kalorama Heights. Absentmindedly, she stuck her hand in the mailbox, routinely checking for any mail. Pulling out a handful of envelopes, she briefly scanned them. One small envelope with chicken scratch handwriting caught her eye. It was too sloppy for the usual junk mail. The handwriting was almost illegible. It was remarkable that the mailman could even read the address. However, whoever wrote the letter knew the least publicized pieces of information about Julia: her middle name. The letter was addressed to "Julia Cherise Morgan, 2441 Tracy Place NW, Washington, DC." Missing was the usual title of "Justice Julia Morgan" as well as the menacing bold "Confidential" that was usually stamped all over the envelope.

When Julia sat down to her usual take-out dinner of a chicken

burrito with jalapeño sauce, she decided to open this envelope first. She tore it open with curiosity as she took the first bite of her burrito.

Dear Julia Cherise,

My letter to you concerns very important and private information. While I am but a simple man living in Mexico, the contents of this letter could change the fate of America. I live in Mexico—in the small city of Nuevo Laredo in Tamaulipas, one of the most beautiful and historic states in Mexico. I know you are familiar with my hometown. I realize you must be surprised by how close I used to live to you, but that is not why I wrote this letter.

I'm sure throughout your childhood, and even now, you wondered who your father was. Why he did not support you and guide you through life? What I am going to tell you next is something you will probably not believe. But you have to trust me: You are my daughter.

Please think about it. Despite better options, you grew up in a small town in Texas by the border that was neither the safest nor the nicest neighborhood. This was because your mother wanted you two to stay as close as possible to me, and I wanted to stay as close as possible to you.

I am so sorry for failing in my role as a parent. I would have done anything to get across the border to see you, but the US is so overprotective of its borders and the immigration process is insanely complex and impossible to pass.

Unfortunately, we will never meet face-to-face. If you are reading this, I'm already dead. I gave a friend two already-sealed letters to mail to you, a week apart, after I died.

I know this all sounds ridiculous, but you'll have to trust me until my next letter comes. My sole possession will be passed down to you next week. It is the only proof I have, and I can only hope that you'll accept the truth.

Your father,
Jorge Anglis

Julia read the letter over and over, first refusing to believe its contents. Absentmindedly, she rubbed her left eye as if this would help her understand the letter better. Just another scammer trying to get me to reply, she thought. But a tiny part of her mind fought back. Then why did he say he was already dead? Ouch! Her left eye started stinging as she realized, too late, that she had rubbed jalapeno sauce into it. She ran to the kitchen sink, her left eye tearing and temporarily blinded by her carelessness. After splashing water onto her eye and then her whole face, she sat down at the table, picking up the letter again. By far, this was not the typical spam she usually received from various political organizations, asking her to do this or that. The decades she had spent in court, hearing case after case, had refined her mind to the point at which she was able to tell what was the truth and what was a lie. And as far-fetched as it sounded, the letter had a tone of truth in it. It was a mix of desperation . . . and regret, sorrow . . . those were emotions that never found their way into the usual political propaganda she received.

As she lay awake in bed, the exhaustion of the day eventually won over the puzzlement of the letter. Julia's eyes slowly closed and she dreamed she was back in the Laredo public library, but this time

she was trapped in the children's reading room by a wall of books.

Chapter Three

A week later, it was the penultimate day before the Supreme Court decision. One would think that all the pressure from the media and constant requests for interviews would push Julia to make up her mind. But here she was, just as undecided on this career-making or career-breaking decision as she had been when the case started half a year ago. The facts were overwhelming and spun through her head like a Ferris wheel that could not stop: 11.1 million undocumented immigrants in the US today. Of those, 50% entered through illegal border crossings. 5.8 million Mexican immigrants were unauthorized. 3.8 billion dollars were spent annually on the Border Patrol budget. 25 billion dollars spent through Mexican remittances.

Julia could not think straight with this eddy of information. And all this was compounded by the political situation she was in. She had been correct about the situation. The other eight judges had already made up their minds. It was unofficially tied four to four. She would be the tiebreaker. So either way, there would be four people yelling at her after the debate, not to mention the president.

The second letter came, as promised, a week later. Julia sat down at her kitchen counter examining the piece of mail carefully with both anticipation and dread. Using her prized silver letter opener engraved with "Supreme Court," she shakily slid open the envelope and pulled out the letter.

Dearest daughter,

This is the second and final letter you will receive from me. I have now been dead for at least two weeks and it is safe to reveal my secret.

I came to Mexico on June 16, 1962. I met your mother for the first and only time on June 14, 1962 in Los Angeles as my brother and I were passing south. It was a fleeting encounter but it is also one that positively changed my life forever. A year later, your mother sent me a letter with a photo of her holding a baby of three months old. I have enclosed this photo for you now. You will recognize your mother's handwriting, your full name and birthdate, and one word: "Ours." I was so happy to finally have someone to live for and love, even if it was only from afar. My double curse is I never got to meet you or your mother again in person before she passed away.

You must be wondering why I could not see you and your mother while you were growing up. Practically, I was not allowed to go to the US. As you well know, it is now very hard for Mexicans to immigrate to the US. But why was I in Mexico? My situation added another layer of complexity. You see, I was #112. Prisoner #112. Prisoner #112 from Alcatraz. My real name is not Jorge Anglis but John Anglin. My brother (your uncle) Clarence Anglin and I were sent to Alcatraz in 1960 for bank robbery. Clarence, Frank Morris, and I are also the infamous threesome who escaped Alcatraz on June 11, 1962. Al Capone, a good friend of mine on Alcatraz, was very well connected and arranged for us to get a boat from Angel Island into The City, and then we "borrowed" a car and drove down to Los Angeles before crossing the border.

As a judge, you know how hard prison can be on people. I

read in the newspapers that you've adopted my perseverance, so you must understand my doggedness at escaping. I have had decades to think about my crimes and I regret them from the bottom of my soul. However, I also feel I have paid my dues.

When planning our escape, becoming Mexican seemed like a brilliant plan. I studied Spanish while on The Rock so my assimilation into my new identity of Mexican-born Jorge Anglis would be smooth. But I did not realize at the time that I would some day actually want to return to the States. Even if I had not been a criminal, simply as a Mexican with no proof of US citizenship (I certainly could not return as John Anglin!) it was not possible for me to immigrate. Being "free" but forced apart from you and your mother by a river and ruthless immigration laws is possibly a living hell worse than a life-sentence on a rock surrounded by the tantalizingly beautiful Bay Area. I have done my time, Julia Cherise, both on Alcatraz and in Mexico.

Take care, my daughter. The world still has an opportunity to change from its horrendous past. You are that changer. You have the power to break the tie.

I end this note by sharing with you the happiest day of my life. You and I did see each other one time when you were about eight. You waved to me across the Rio Grande and I waved back. Your fleeting hand motion and shy smile have kept me going all these decades.

Lovingly,
John Anglin, your father

Astounded by what she had just read, Julia sat unflinching in her chair. Her phone rang. The oven timer went off. But her whirling thoughts were impervious to these trivial distractions. Was this man really her father? Yes, it seemed so given that he had her baby photo and it was clearly her mother's handwriting on it. Was the man really John Anglin, the infamous Alcatraz escapee? Here, her logically trained mind was less sure. Could it ever be proven? Did DNA samples exist in the 1960s so Anglin's could be tested against hers? Perhaps the letter should be tested for fingerprints? Julia thought as she hastily dropped it on to the table in front of her. Then questions came flooding so fast she could not keep track of them. Did they really escape Alcatraz by floating in the chilly waters of the San Francisco Bay? Did all three of them make it to land? How did he meet her mother in Los Angeles? Did her mother help him escape to Mexico? What did he do in Mexico all this time? Why hadn't her mother told her anything? Should Julia tell the press? Should she tell the FBI? Should she tell the president? And finally, if John Anglin was really her father, would she be kicked off the Supreme Court as the daughter of a convicted criminal?

By three o'clock in the morning, there was only one issue that her mind could grasp and attempt to address. Even if the man who had written the two letters wasn't her father, he had made a key point that she just had to accept. Whether she was kicked off the court or not, she literally had the power to break the tie. How the man knew to write that, metaphorically or literally, was something she would never know. She thought about the letter's last few lines even harder. Which way was she going to break the tie? The line "The world still has an opportunity to change from its horrendous past" resonated even more deeply. She remembered Laredo. She remembered the violence from Nuevo Laredo. Then she remembered what her mother had always told her: *Welcome people, Julia, even if they aren't part of*

your community. Her mother's words of wisdom as well as her secrecy around who her father was finally all made sense. Julia had a plan.

Chapter Four

The next day, Julia marched up the steps of the Supreme Court. Her confident strides echoing against the marble floor hid the turmoil inside of her. As always at the end of a case, the nine justices walked into the secluded voting room, closed to all but them. They all sat down around a wooden table, with anticipating excitement for what would come. Following tradition, they arranged themselves from most to least senior, Julia being the last justice to sit down. There were no clerks inside; only the justices would know about the vote. Going around the table, the justices spoke their final word of the case.

For!

Against!

Against!

Against!

For!

Against!

For!

For!

It was tied. As Julia had suspected, she would be the deciding vote. And even more, as the most junior justice, she would be heckled by the senior justices . . . that voted for the case.

Against!

The justices were astonished. Julia could see it as eight pairs of wide-opened eyes bore into her. The scowls on the brows of the four supporters made her head hurt. The grins on the mouths of the four others made her want to stand up and yell.

Would she be ostracized for her vote as well as her background? Would she lose her job? Only time would tell. But Julia realized her heart felt lighter. She hadn't felt this happy since she was a child, standing on the banks of the Rio Grande with Alejandra, waving to people, perhaps even her own relatives, in Nuevo Laredo. She, Julia Cherise Morgan, had been the tiebreaker on the United States Supreme Court on a decision that would forever change the course of US history and its relationship with its neighboring countries.

She knew now that the most important day of her life was not the day the president had called her, but the day that the letters had arrived. The letters that changed her life and pushed her to break the tie. Her one vote had decided the fate of the entire Supreme Court's verdict, which would protect and improve the lives of millions of people. She had finally made a difference to the world.

Building toward a Twist

Dear Reader,

I really enjoyed reading Amanvir's poem, "The Twilight's Critters." Amanvir has a great, natural sense of rhythm as well as fun, surprising rhymes—two very important tools while writing poetry.

Amanvir's first stanza (a.k.a. poem-paragraph) sounds like a wise-but-neutral narrator ("The sun will soon set, / Little child, get ready for bed"), the kind of voice that might narrate a fairy tale. That's why the change to a humorous, more casual tone in the second stanza ("The name's Mr. Owl") is such a wonderful surprise—we as readers were given an expectation about the narrator would be like, and then this narrator was totally different!

One way to take an already-great poem and bring it to the next level is to add an element of surprise again at the very end. There are *so* many things that make great poems great, but one of my favorites is building toward a twist, or a "turn." (In poetry-speak, this is sometimes called a "volta.") Amanvir's first stanza sets up readers to expect a wise, neutral, fairy-tale narrator—and then his second stanza makes us laugh by changing that narrator's tone. Just like that surprise between two stanzas, you can think about what your *whole poem* makes readers expect, so that you can surprise your readers again with something different in the last stanza or even the very last line. Amanvir's new version of the poem plays with readers' expectations of Mr. Owl as a well-mannered authority figure—and then surprises us with his wild (and kind of gross) appetite.

Probably the most important (and most fun) way to become a more masterful writer is by reading *a lot*. Read examples of poems and stories that do what you're trying to do. The following poems do a great job of building toward a twist, and they're all available online if you want to check them out:

- "Porcupines" by Marilyn Singer (a *very* short poem that still includes an expectation and a surprise!)
- "The Dentist and the Crocodile" by Roald Dahl

- "Eating Words" by Katherine Hauth
- "Dirty Face" by Shel Silverstein

Can you figure out where the twist begins in each one? What kind of expectation did each poet give you during each poem, and how did that expectation become a surprise at the end? Once you can identify the trick, you can use it yourself!

Happy reading and revising,
Sarah Lyn Rogers

Sarah Lyn Rogers is a Pushcart-nominated writer and editor from the San Francisco Bay Area. She is the author of *Inevitable What*, a poetry collection focused on magic and rituals, which is being translated into Chinese by a faraway pen pal named Jane. As Fiction Editor for *The Rumpus*, Sarah reads hundreds of stories by adults every year and publishes the ones that strike a nice balance between funny and heartbreaking. By the time you read this, she should finally be done writing her first novel.

Amanvir Parhar

Amanvir is in the sixth grade at Warm Springs Elementary School. He loves geometry and will devote his time to math. He also loves poetry and writing in general. In his free time, Amanvir is thinking of ideas for new stories and poems.

Sarah Lyn Rogers: How long have you been writing?
Amanvir Parhar: I have been writing for roughly four years.

Q: What is your favorite genre to write, and about what kinds of things do you like to write most?
A: I love speculative fiction and mysteries. I sometimes write about animals, famous people, or my own eccentric characters.

Q: Who are your favorite authors and/or favorite books?
A: I like *The Westing Game* by Ellen Raskin, a mystery, and *Echo* by Pam Muñoz Ryan.

Q: What tool did you learn from this editing process that you can use forever now?
A: For my poetry, I have learned how to keep my poem's beat count and add a taste of mystery.

Q: What are you writing next?
A: I am thinking of writing fictional story involving time.

The Twilight's Critters

by

Amanvir Parhar

The sun will soon set,
Little child, get ready for bed,
Your day is about done,
Mine, though, has just begun.

Why, sorry, mister or miss,
My manners have been foul,
I haven't even introduced myself,
The name's Mr. Owl.

I am a creature of the night,
A bird with marvelous eyesight,
It gives me quite a good view,
Of the caribous and the kinkajous!

But when the sun is up in the sky,
On our beds we will lie,

Then we shall be sound asleep,

Until the sundown, owls will not cheep.

So long, little tyke,

I'll be on my way,

I'll fetch some food that I like,

Why, I need to get those rats, the rats that are gray!

Rounding out the Ending

Briana Mitchell mentored Lily Shi through a revision
focused on what lasting impression to leave in Lily's story,
"The Unlikely Superhero."

When I read "The Unlikely Superhero," I was struck by how delightful and action-packed the story was. I couldn't wait to begin digging in and revising it with Lily!

I was very impressed with the way she developed both the plot and the characters in her story! She clearly has a knack for giving each character his or her own distinct voice, and motivating the action in the story so that it moves the plot along. I wanted to focus on rounding out the ending of Lily's story. The ending of a story is the last thing we, as authors, leave with the reader. It's our chance to leave a lasting impression, and decide how we want the reader to feel as they finish our story.

Lily and I went through three steps as she revised:

First: I asked her to think about every step of this journey that Noah and his siblings are on. Making a list sometimes helps! We thought specifically about the end of this journey: the battle with the Reptile Lord onwards. Now, not all of the steps and details that Lily thought of made it into her manuscript. If they did, we'd probably have a full-length novel by now! However, I wanted to make sure she could see every detail, hear every conversation, and envision each exciting bit of action. That way, she could convey it to her readers.

Second: Lily decided which of those steps and details are important for the reader to know. She took a look at what she already had written down in her draft, and compared that to all the details she had just conjured up. Then, she asked herself: Were there any new details she'd like to include? Anything that can paint a clearer picture, build a smoother ending, or make a moment more colorful for the reader?

Third: Lastly, Lily picked at least three spots towards the end of her story where she could add details that will help the reader better understand this story and follow what happens to the amazing characters she has created. She spent a lot of time thinking from the reader's perspective and asking herself, "How can I take the clear image I see in my head, and paint a word-picture for the reader?"

I am so impressed with both Lily's writing skills and the progress she made throughout this revision process! I couldn't be more proud and excited to see this story published. It represents lots of laughter, hard work, and even more imagination. I hope you enjoy "The Unlikely Superhero" and are as inspired by this story as I am!

Happy Reading,
Briana Mitchell

Briana Mitchell has always had a love for stories! Be it through theatre, writing, or good old spooky stories by the campfire, the power of storytelling has been a constant in her life. Briana deeply believes that play and story go hand in hand, and has been inspired by the Society of Young Inklings pedagogy. She has been involved with SYI as a mentor and instructor since 2015. Briana holds a Bachelor of Arts in theatre and Spanish from Santa Clara University, and currently acts with local theatre companies around the Bay Area.

Lily Shi

Lily is a third grader at Argonaut Elementary School in Saratoga, California. She loves to dance, play soccer, and draw. She reads every day and writes stories for fun. She also likes to solve interesting math and logic puzzles. Someday, she would like to invent robots that will do our work for us. Lily hopes you enjoy her story!

Briana Mitchell: How did you come up with the idea for your story?
Lily Shi: Well, I wanted to write about a person who isn't very good at what he does, but is very brave. And being brave alone makes him successful. And then I thought about superheroes, and I got my idea for this story.

Q: Have you written other stories? Or is this your first?
A: I write a lot of stories for fun, and I wrote a story for last year's Inklings Book Contest, but I didn't get in. I was a finalist, though!

Q: How did you feel when you were selected this year for the Inklings Book Contest?
A: I felt really good and excited!

Q: Now that you have been through the IBC process, what's your favorite part?

A: My favorite part was submitting the story and being a part of the contest. Because last year, I didn't get in—so when I got in this year, I was really excited!

Q: In what way do you think your story improved through this process?
A: My story has a lot more detail and conversation and emotion that makes it easier for the reader to understand.

Q: Do you have any advice for other young authors?
A: Even though you think your first draft may be bad, you can always revise it to make it better.

The Unlikely Superhero

by

Lily Shi

The bank was quiet and peaceful. Every so often, the doors would open and a person would walk in or out. People spoke quietly with each other if they spoke at all. The marble floors were polished until they gleamed. The walls were as smooth as the floors, and the windows shone until they seemed invisible. The golden pillars stretched towards the tall dome ceiling. The wooden counter always stayed neat and tidy, and seldom were there random things lying around.

This was what the bank looked like every day.

But one day, a sunny and cloudless Monday, at precisely 8:42 a.m., there was an out-of-the-ordinary sound.

Crash!

The windows shattered, scattering shards of glass onto the floor. A gang of robbers wearing black suits and masks stormed in and held up guns.

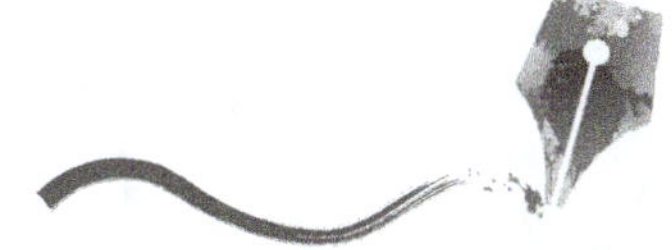

People started screaming and running for the exit.

"Silence!" barked the leader. "Silence or I'll shoot!" The people fell silent.

"Now on the ground with your hands over your head," he ordered. "And no talking!"

The citizens followed his orders obediently.

Next, the robbers pointed their guns at the tellers.

"Empty the safe! And no funny business or I blow you into pieces!"

The trembling tellers did as they were told.

If the citizens weren't lying face down on the ground, they would have seen a silhouette of a boy wearing a cape and striking a heroic pose against the other window. They would have thought that rescue had come until they realized that the boy could not open the window.

Then finally, with a strong tug, the window crashed to the floor. The robbers turned around and pointed their guns at the boy. Then they saw who it was and put down their guns and sighed.

"Never fear, 'cause Noah is here!" the boy yelled. Then he slipped on his cape and tumbled off the windowsill and onto the ground.

The robbers snickered and the citizens' eager smiles turned to sighs of disappointment.

Noah stood up and glared at the robbers, his cheeks red.

"I see you've escaped prison," he said, in a voice that was obviously deeper than his normal one.

Noah was a ten-year-old boy with messy dark hair. He wore a red suit with a huge yellow lightning bolt in the middle. He had a matching red cape, and he was barefooted.

The lead robber turned to his henchmen. "Get him. But don't waste your bullets. He's not worth it."

"Oh yeah?" Noah fumed. "I'm worth all the bullets you got!"

Then he activated his power. His hair crackled with electricity. Sparks flew from his hands as he rubbed them together.

He grinned, then somersaulted over to the lead robber and tapped him with his index finger.

"Ouch," the robber snorted. "That almost hurt a little."

Noah ignored him and cartwheeled over to the other robbers. He shocked them too, but this seemed to irritate the robbers instead of harming them.

"I changed my mind," the lead robber said. "Shoot him."

"That's more like it!" Noah yelled.

He jumped into the air. His flying did not contain the grace of an eagle or an owl, but the grace of a baby bird. Every few seconds he would fall down. Then he would surge up again. Sometimes, he would fall sideways, or backwards, but he would stay in the air.

Because of his erratic flight pattern, it became harder to shoot Noah, so the robbers used the butts of their guns to knock him out of the sky. They tied him up to a chair and gagged him. Then they continued with their robbing.

With their duffel bags filled with money, they were about to leave, when there was another crash in the roof. The rest of the superheroes had arrived!

"Great," muttered the first robber.

The first superhero had a dark blue suit and a black mask. He was sixteen and barefoot. The tips of his black hair were frozen and

white. He wore a light blue cape, and he was standing on a floor of ice. Everywhere he went, ice formed under his feet, so he could walk in the air. His skin was as pale as snow.

The second superhero wore a bright neon yellow suit and a black mask. She was fourteen with long red hair that was styled into two long braids. She had a yellow skirt and a yellow cape. The ends of her braids were circling round and round, and it propelled her through the air.

The third superhero wore a dark green suit with a slightly different shade of green for his cape. Instead of a mask, he wore large sunglasses. He had red hair, like the girl, and he was thirteen. Sprouting out of his back were two huge feathery white wings that helped him fly.

The three superheroes landed. A circle of ice appeared from where the first superhero was standing. The second superhero's braids stopped circling, but still stayed in the air and crept closer to the robbers menacingly. The third superhero's wings disappeared, and instantly, a cooler look emerged as he crossed his arms and glared.

Noah rolled his eyes at his siblings' grand entrance.

"Luke. Guinevere. Zane," the lead robber addressed them.

"Robbers. Robbers. And even more robbers," Luke, the oldest, growled.

"I see you've come back to save you little brother," the robber smirked.

A muffled sound of protestation came from Noah.

The superheroes ignored the sound.

"Only after we're done with you," Guinevere, the girl, replied.

The robbers made a run for it. All seven of them crammed through the windows.

"Oh, no you don't," Guinevere muttered.

She reached out her arm. It stretched and stretched through the window out of sight, then came back with a handful of robbers. She set them down on the ground, and her arm went back to normal length.

The robbers held up their guns.

"Shoot at me," Zane said calmly.

Boom!

As the bullet passed through the air, Zane morphed into an ant. The bullet missed him and struck the wall.

Suddenly, the air was filled with the sound of guns firing. Luke made a wall of ice in front of him. The bullets bounced harmlessly on the wall and fell off. Guinevere twisted herself into different types of shapes to dodge the bullets. Zane remained as an ant and waited on the ground.

Soon, the robbers' bullets ran out. They dropped the guns and charged at the superheroes. Zane turned into a wall. The only thing remaining the same about his human form was his sunglasses. He knocked the robbers charging at him unconscious. Luke froze the robbers mid-step. And Guinevere tripped the robbers with her long hair. Zane morphed into a cage. Guinevere's hair and arms stretched out, grabbed all the robbers, and tossed them inside the cage. She locked the door before the robbers could run. Luke was phoning the police.

Then, they untied Noah from the chair while all the citizens thanked them and the bankers put the money back. Zane transformed

into a dragon for Noah to ride on, and they all flew home.

❧ ❧ ❧

Back at the house, Luke explained to their inventor and creator, or, as they like to call him, their dad, how Noah had sneaked out of the house and tried to save the bank.

"Noah, Noah, Noah, Noah," their dad sighed, shaking his head. "How am I ever going to stop you?"

"It's not fair!" Noah shouted. "Luke and Guinevere and Zane fought against criminals and villains when they were my age!"

"Noah," their dad sighed. "You're just a late bloomer. Your powers aren't fully fledged yet! You might get hurt!"

"I can zap people and shock them," Noah protested. "And I can fly!"

Luke, who was eating ice cubes and doing push-ups, looked at Noah.

"Your zapping and shocking barely does anything! When your powers are fully fledged, you should be able to electrify people. But not now!"

"Well, make it fledge faster!"

Guinevere, who was reading a magazine held up by her feet while her outstretched arms styled her hair, looked up. "You can't make your powers fledge faster! And plus, you still need to work on your flying."

"My flying is fine!" Noah protested.

"No, it isn't," Zane, who was looking into a magazine and

practicing morphing into the items that he saw, said. "You can only go a few feet up into the air, your flying patterns are clumsy and erratic, and you can't even glide."

"I just want to help people," Noah muttered.

"How can you help people if you can't help yourself?" Guinevere said.

Noah stayed silent.

"Go play with your batteries," Luke ordered. "I can't stand whining."

Noah sighed, then started building structures out of the broken batteries.

Soon, he stopped and sat on the couch, thinking.

It wasn't fair! Noah knew that he could be a great superhero. He had the courage. He wouldn't chicken out on fighting monsters. Why were his powers not fully fledged? Anger boiled up inside him. It was stupid to ask permission to be great! Was there something he could do to make his powers fledge faster?

He was about to ask his dad when the radio beeped.

"Paris is under attack of the Reptile Lord! He is currently on top of the Eiffel Tower for unknown reasons. He has done nothing yet, but has caused fear and chaos."

Luke jumped up. "Let's go. We can't waste any time."

Guinevere and Zane stood up. So did Noah.

"You're staying right here," Noah's father said firmly. "You're grounded!"

"*What*?" Noah yelled. "How will I fight criminals and villains?"

"You won't," Noah's dad replied. "You'll stay right here while your siblings take down the Reptile Lord."

"But . . ." Noah stuttered.

"No buts."

Noah gaped at his father. His father looked away. Noah stomped up to his room in a rage.

I must improve my powers! Noah was determined. *I will not stop until my powers are fully fledged!* He started to activate his powers. He zapped everything in the room he could find. He flew in and out of his window. He sent electricity through the wires in his small TV that he kept in his room. He worked so long without interruption that he was surprised when the radio beeped.

"The Reptile Lord has captured the superheroes Luke, Guinevere, and Zane! Repeat: The Reptile Lord has captured the superheroes Luke, Guinevere, and Zane!"

Noah stood frozen for a few seconds.

Now the city would fall!

But a voice silently called to him.

But you secretly wished they would fail!

Noah tried to push that voice away, but it always came back. It grew bigger and bigger.

You wanted them to fail so you could go defeat the Reptile Lord!

Noah couldn't push the voice away.

Suddenly, another thought popped into his head. His siblings were captured, and if the Reptile Lord had his way, they probably would be . . . Noah couldn't imagine it. He realized that this wasn't about proving himself anymore. He had to go confront the Reptile Lord for his family. For the people of Earth.

He rushed down the stairs and hugged his dad. "I'm going to

rescue Luke, Guinevere, and Zane," he whispered in his ear.

"But . . ." he stuttered.

"No buts. And remember me. Forever."

And with that, Noah rushed out of the door.

Once Noah arrived at the Eiffel Tower, he jumped up the side of it using his not-so-developed flying skills. When he finally reached the top, his hands were bruised and his feet were bleeding.

The Reptile Lord looked horrible! He had the head of a crocodile and a tail of a snake. His front legs were like a turtle and the back legs like a lizard. His eyes were like a chameleon's. His two assistants looked like lizards, except they were standing up and wearing glasses.

Then he saw his siblings. They were tied to the side of the tower with ropes that were thick and blue. The ropes were also glowing, so Noah guessed that they were magic ropes that took away his siblings' superpowers.

Then his siblings saw him.

"Noah!" Luke gasped.

"What are you doing?" Guinevere whispered.

"Get out of here!" Zane screamed.

The Reptile Lord turned around and fixed Noah in his burning gaze.

"Well," the Reptile Lord hissed. "This is perfect! I have all four superheroes under my power. Of course, *you* won't be any use. You don't have fully fledged powers."

Noah's hair crackled with electricity and his body flew with sparks.

"I'll just have my assistants take you down," the Reptile Lord

continued. He laughed and nodded at the lizards.

The lizards stepped menacingly towards Noah. Noah's eyes widened, and he backed up and hit a barrel of water. The lizards laughed when they saw his concern. They started running towards him. Noah thought fast. He tipped over the barrel of water. Then he touched it with his finger and the lizards, who were staring in horror at his crackling hair and the sparks flying from his body, fell dead.

Luke cheered. Zane gaped at him. And Guinevere uncovered her eyes. The Reptile Lord sighed at him a long sigh.

"I guess I'll have to do this myself," he hissed, then with a surprising speed, he ran at Noah and rammed him off the tower.

Guinevere screamed.

"You monster!" Luke shouted.

"Haven't you done enough already?" Zane yelled.

"He was just a little boy!" Guinevere cried.

The Reptile Lord laughed. "You'll get over it. Once the Emerald Snake Eyes I stole from the museum activates to its full power, all living creatures will be turned into reptiles! And you will be my first testers!"

Guinevere was still crying. The Reptile Lord droned on and on about how he would rule the world. None of them noticed the bright light that was growing bigger by the second. With the light came a crackling sound. Guinevere looked up. The Reptile Lord stopped talking.

Their eyes adjusted to the light.

"Noah!" Zane shouted.

"You're back!" cried Guinevere.

"And powerful!" added Luke.

Noah's eyes were gleaming with a shining light. With his

powers fully fledged, he sent a blast of electricity towards the Reptile Lord. The Reptile Lord fell over and let go of the Emerald Snake Eyes, which fell to the ground. Then Noah sent blasts towards the ropes that were holding his siblings hostage. The ropes sizzled and fell apart where he had hit them. Noah had a huge smile on his face.

"You may be able to defeat me," the Reptile Lord wheezed, "But you will not be able to defeat my army!"

He made a sound that was between a growl, a hiss, a grunt, a croak, and a snort. Soon, an army of millions of reptiles were speeding up the Eiffel Tower. The horrified citizens gasped when they saw the monsters the Reptile Lord had created. Noah's eyebrows shot to the top of his head and his eyes widened—his siblings had once told him that the Reptile Lord could summon reptiles whenever he needed to, but he had never imagined it to look like *this*.

The superheroes glanced at each other and their eyes met. Then, in a series of head-nods and hand gestures that lasted a few seconds, they had a plan. Luke froze the part of the Eiffel Tower that the reptiles were traveling on. Zane turned into a fire and burned the ice so that the top half of the ice turned into water. Guinevere, taking a step back, lashed out her hand, grabbed Zane, and hauled him back up before the reptiles could reach him. Then, Noah sent a bolt of lightning at the water. Instantly, all reptiles fell dead.

There was silence.

Then the crowd started cheering. Clapping, whooping, whistling, and shouting could be heard for more than ten miles away from the superheroes. The cheering lasted for four hours. The superheroes smiled and waved at the crowd. After a long group hug, the older siblings praised and apologized to Noah. Suddenly,

Noah remembered that his dad was waiting for them at home. So, the superheroes waved goodbye to the crowd and left.

At their house, their father hugged them until the breath was squeezed out of them.

"Noah," Noah's dad said to him sternly after the extra special dinner that he prepared for Noah and his siblings, "I can't say I was happy about your going out of the house after you were grounded. Yet it all turned out well, with you saving the world and such."

Noah's dad's voice softened as he continued. "I'm *very* sorry that I discouraged you from being a true superhero. You were right. You are a superhero even without powers. It is your courage that makes you a hero, not your superpowers. Never let what others say affect what you want to do. I will always be on your side. You are special and you cannot be replaced. Use my words as a shield against what others say. You can do everything."

So, from that day on, Noah became known as the world's greatest superhero. He was always the first to arrive at a distressing scene, no matter how terrifying the villain was, and he was never defeated in a fight. And his siblings never envied him for being greater than them, for they knew that he deserved it.

Setting for Impact

Erica Morgan helped Samuel Teoh emphasize setting details to ground readers in his story, "The Battle in the Body."

Dear Reader,

Stories can take us to other worlds. We can visit other planets, climb into Icelandic volcanoes, take submarines to the depths of the sea, or live on a Swiss mountainside. That ability to transport people to places they might never be able to go in real life is part of what makes fiction so special. In "The Battle in the Body," Sam takes us to a very special setting indeed—inside ourselves.

Sam has created a story that is partially set within the human body as Cells and Germs do battle for dominance. It is a fascinating read for anyone who's ever fought off an "evil" illness and emerged victorious!

The main goal that we had in editing the story was to give

the setting greater impact. We did that partially through small changes (like adding names and details), but mainly by letting ourselves imagine we were really in the story. We thought strategically about where skirmishes would take place, what zones would be safe, and what areas of the body were the most vital. We also worked out the best times for perspective shifts and changes in setting. We called this strategic approach setting for impact.

Sam started out with a very good idea for a story. He then put pen to paper and worked hard on a solid draft. After that, he sat down and examined his choices. He changed certain things, and decided not to change others. Each step of that process helped solidify the story into one of intrigue, adventure, and humor. I could not be more proud of him for his creativity, skill, and hard work throughout it all.

Remember, when you work on your own stories, having a wonderful idea is only the first step. Following the path to a great story will take time and effort, but that time can be spent with creativity and laughter, and that effort can be a wonderful opportunity to grow.

Happy writing!
Erica Morgan

Erica Morgan is a lover of fiction, an avid producer and consumer of poetry, a longtime Young Inklings instructor, and a very questionable cook! She believes that stories are a big part of how we understand the world, and that by sharing our stories (even the ones from our imaginations!) we can come to understand one another much more profoundly.

Samuel Teoh

Sam is a big fan of reading, writing, drawing, and playing! He wants to be a writer, adventurer, scientist, or architect when he grows up. Maybe all four! He would love to have a dog someday, and would probably name him "?" or "Roald Dog."

Erica Morgan: Why do you enjoy writing?
Samuel Teoh: It's fun. I get to write whatever I want and write about what I think.

Q: What made you choose this story for the Inklings Book Contest?
A: I like battles.

Q: How do you come up with your ideas?
A: I was reading something that had a lot of battles—like *The Magic School Bus*, but longer—and that gave me the idea for this story. Sometimes I just think things up.

Q: Do you like to read? What are your favorite books?
A: My favorite books are Harry Potter, Percy Jackson, Narnia, *The Hobbit*, *Matilda*, *Charlie and the Chocolate Factory*, *Charlie and the Great Glass Elevator*, *James and the Giant Peach*, *The Land of Stories*, and *Fantastic Mr. Fox*.

Q: Who do you enjoy sharing your stories with?

A: No one usually.

Q: Are you working on a new story?

A: I am working on a story that is like a sequel to this one. Also, I am working on a new one that I haven't named yet.

The Battle in the Body

by

Samuel Teoh

Andrew's Plan

My friend, Alan, had a flu.

When I went to his house, he said that there was a battle inside him and I shook my head and said that it wasn't true but he said, "There is a battle between myself and the Germs." He said, "Do you want to hear my story?"

I nodded and said curiously, "Okay." Then he began.

The Germs were invading the territory of the Cells.

Billions of Cells were already dead, though the war had only just started. The Brain was the worst battle zone. Millions of both dead and live Cells and Germs flowed out of the nose. In the hippocampus, where the emotions live, Germs scurried around while the immense

Cells tried to squash them. The Cells had the advantage, though there was still no sign of victory.

But the Germs were strong—strong enough the fight the Cells.

Even though the ginormous Cells were greatly supplied with celery and carrots, the nutritious supplies soon began to shorten. Most of the generals and some of the bravest Cells died.

The Germs bombed the Cells' military bases with planes and tanks, and the Cells were forced to retreat to their headquarters in the vocal cords. It was safe, but there were frequent vibrations that felt like earthquakes.

The Germs had killed most of the Cells and it was clear the Cells were losing and the Germs were gaining victory.

"So, the Germs won and the Cells lost?" I asked, disappointed that the Germs were victorious.

Alan held up his hand. "Wait till the end, Anthony," he said.

So, I waited.

And he continued.

One clever Cell named Andrew had not given up and had made plans for victory.

The next morning, he got up and told his friends the plan he had thought of the night before.

"We will invade tonight," Andrew said as he pulled out his

map of the enemy military base in the aorta that he had stolen from a guard. "The Germs will go to sleep. Then we will set on fire the exits and entrances of the Germs' military base."

"What will we do?" asked five other Cell friends in unison as they entered the room.

"I haven't thought of it yet," said Andrew slowly.

"I have an idea," said one of Andrew's closest friends, Fred. "You could wait outside and kill whoever escapes."

"All right," they said.

Alan paused.

"Did the plan work?" I asked.

"I'm not sure," he said slowly and shook his head. "I don't know the end of it."

Just then, Helen May, Alan's mom, walked into the room with water and vegetable sticks.

"What are you doing, boys?" Helen asked.

"I'm telling the story, Mom. You know, the Battle in the Body," Alan said.

"Go on," Helen told us as she took a spot on the bed. "I didn't mean to interrupt."

"I don't know if Fred's plan worked, Mom," he told her and shrugged.

"Okay," Helen said, "I'll tell the story from here."

Pandora's Plan

After the Cells got into their hiding places, something went terribly wrong and most of the sneaky Germs escaped. The Germs had an emergency exit underground in a tunnel.

The Cells were horrified when their Germ prey was suddenly behind them, creepy and violent. They looked to each other with wide eyes, and prepared for the great battle they knew was coming. They sharpened their swords and prepared to throw their spears at the Germs flooding down on them.

Even though Andrew's friends fought bravely, they all died. Despite their defeat, they managed to save his life, though.

He made his way home to his apartment in the Left Lung. Andrew gave up his plans of victory, thinking that the Germs would win.

When Andrew's sister, Pandora, heard of this, she told her brother that she had a plan. She took Andrew's map of the enemy base and told him her plan. Andrew was awestruck.

"It's a crazy plan," Andrew said. "I'll work on it."

Andrew got his neighbors together and told them Pandora's plan.

Surprisingly, many agreed to it. The tanks were set to invade the military camp in Wrist Forest while planes bombed the military bases and headquarters near Hamstring Harbor.

The Cells were supposed to dig trenches at the end of underground escape ways.

☖ ◊ ☖

When she stopped to take a breath, we heard my mom call out.

"Wait!" I called back at her. "Can I finish the story please?"

"What story?" she asked as she appeared in Alan's bedroom doorway with her purse.

"Hi, Helen," she said as she took a seat next to Alan's mom. "What story are you talking about?"

"You know, Theodora," Alan's mom said, "the Battle in the Body?"

"Oh, yes," my mom said. "Father told of it before."

"You know the story?" I asked. "The Battle in the Body?"

"Yes, honey," she said. "Your grandfather told us the story before when we were young."

"Can you tell us it then?" Alan spoke up. "We were at Pandora's plan."

"Oh, all right." My mom grinned. "I'll tell my part."

The Battle of Ernest, Big Toe

Pandora's plan did work—for a while.

The Cells soon began to tire and the Germs had gathered into the most ferocious army—and their last squads. Most of the Germs began to gather around the Wrist Forest to blow up everything in it. But the worst battle wasn't there. It was in a quiet town of Big Toe called Ernest.

It all started when a boy called Darius called the Germ King a name. A Germite spy was on the rooftop of the church listening to the

insult and he quickly told the message to the king. The king, Aniamus, wasn't the forgiving type so he got his army together and went to ambush the town.

When the town heard this, they were terrified and quickly executed Darius on the spot. They hired a famous general to fight for them. The general gathered all the men in the town. It made up to seven billion Cells, and they went to battle the Germs.

Even though the army of the Germites was strong and ferocious, the Cells were greatly skilled and ready for battle. The Cells' armor was invincible and their weapons were strong and did a great amount of damage.

Little by little the Germites fled out of the city and the Germites' general was killed in battle. In the battle, a house was burned down and forty Germs were killed in it. After the Germites retreated, the town was filled with hundreds of dead bodies of the Germs.

The Germs had lost many men in battle and approximately three billion Germs had died and eight hundred Cells had been killed during the war. Darius's dad was also killed in the war and his mom died shortly after of grief.

The Cells had won a great victory over the Germs and they were honored for it.

"So, the Cells won, right?" I asked.

My mom's eyes twinkled. "They didn't win yet, just wait."

"Okay," I said, still unsatisfied at the answer.

The Battle at Elbow Island

There was another victory after the Battle of Ernest. The battle was fought in a town called Joint on an island called Elbow Island.

The battle wasn't great in the beginning; it was just a tiny skirmish between the Cells and a bit of Pollen. Just as they began to fight, there was a great wind and the battle was over. It got solved with a sneeze.

The Cells were winning!

The Defeat of the Germs

Though the campaigns of the Cells were victorious, there was another great battle to determine who would win.

The Cells' general, Wadcliff Tredstorm, and the Germs' general, Louisiana Emmit, planned the battle and the attacks. Tredstorm marched his army up the mount and camped for two days in a dark cave. Emmit took her army and came to the top of the mount and camped there for two days.

Tredstorm then ordered his army to bring their shields and swords and some guns and marched up the mount. Tredstorm told his army to split up into four combinations and attack from the four sides of the mountain. Tredstorm's troops armored and shielded themselves and shot up the mountain, shooting with their guns.

Tredstorm's army trapped Emmit's army on the hill.

Emmit was killed in the battle and when the army saw their leader was dead, Emmit's army fled down the mount and accidentally drowned themselves in the lake.

The Germs had lost a very important battle and the Cells were victorious.

The army of Cells pushed the Germs out of the land and executed all of them at Saint Jone's River.

∽ ●◇ ∽

"That was kind of gross," I said.

"That was totally awesome," Alan corrected.

"Right," Mom said. She turned to me, serious again. "We'd better get home."

"Why?" I asked.

"Dad's waiting," she told me.

"I hope you feel better," I told Alan.

"You bet I will," he said with a grin. He waved at me as we parted.

Clarity

Malar Ganapathiappan mentored Ann Yang, showing her where and how to make her imaginative ideas clear to readers in her story, "How the Infamous Hot Pepper Came to Be!"

Dear Reader,

Ann's story—"How the Infamous Hot Pepper Came to Be!"—is such an entertaining and fun story with amusing animal characters!

For Ann's revision, we focused on clarity. She had a unique idea to explain an interesting phenomenon. Since the events were so imaginative, clarity was especially important to allow the reader to fully enjoy the story.

In order to develop clarity, we first discussed logical questions. How did the peppers get into the bathroom? How did the peppers suddenly come to life in Squeak's bathroom? How did the peppers meet the gopher and employ him? How does the gopher immediately know they became spicy when the fly bit them? When she added some details to answer these questions, she appreciated that she'd given her reader a clearer mental picture of the story.

"Show not tell" is commonly used advice. Ann worked on this in her story by thinking deeper about the personality of Squeak the mouse and showing it through his reactions to the peppers. She had done well describing the events with colorful words. Using language strongly like that meant additional adverbs weren't necessary. In fact, they became "telling" when she already "showed" through action descriptions. For example, shifting in your seat, twiddling your fingers, or tapping a foot are actions which *show* impatience. So the word impatient doesn't need to be used as well. Taking out any unnecessary words polishes and refines the story.

One other thing Ann played with was mixing up sentence length so there was a break from long sentences. When there are long sentences throughout, there is little time for the reader to pause and catch up with what's going on. Having a lot of commas can get confusing also. Shorter sentences can draw attention to important details or events. It is interesting to see how small changes can make big impacts on clarity.

Malar Ganapathiappan

Malar Ganapathiappan finds joy in stories and loves sharing inspiration and creativity with others. She earned a psychology BA summa cum laude. While not reading, writing, or instructing, she enjoys exploring the outdoors.

Ann Yang

Ann is currently a sixth grader at Pleasanton Middle School (PMS). Some of her hobbies include writing short stories, biking, and playing with her playful and silly dog, Sydney. Ann's favorite animals are octopuses and dogs. In the future, Ann hopes to publish a book, and become an engineer/inventor.

Malar Ganapathiappan: How did you get the idea for your story?

Ann Yang: I remember going to the library at school and the librarian would tell stories. I came across a certain story about how a rabbit and carrot became friends. I wrote this story a long time ago when I was younger but I changed it when I decided to make it into an actual story. For Squeak, in fourth/fifth grade, teachers read a lot of books about mice and their personalities. I thought the idea of a mouse in the stories was really interesting.

Q: How do you feel about your story after the changes?

A: I feel like the changes made the story a lot more accurate and you can understand it better. Adding Squeak's personality makes you understand him better. Turning the gopher into a farmer is more reasonable because then you can see why he would talk to some random peppers.

Q: Why do you enjoy writing?

A: Most of my ideas spawned off when I was younger. My mom used to write stories with me. When I was little, I wrote a version of *The Little Mermaid*. My mom did the writing and I drew pictures. Those times with my mom really made a difference. They inspired me to keep writing. Now I write a short story every day. Plus, I had a really good writing teacher and I learned a lot from her. There was a time when I didn't like writing essays, but she made writing more enjoyable.

Q: Do you think you'll write more stories with animal characters?

A: Yes. I think I'll write a few more stories with human characters but more with animal characters. Most stories out there are about humans and sometimes when writing about animals, you can give them new personalities instead of human personalities. Right now, I'm writing a story about a hermit crab and a seagull.

How the Infamous Hot Pepper Came to Be!

by

Ann Yang

In the long, grassy fields of the wide, barren land, tucked away into a corner, was a tiny hut. Steam billowed out from the miniature chimney, where the sweet, aromatic smell of peppers was extremely strong. Inside the hut was an auburn mouse named Squeak. He bustled around his kitchen, cooking a nice meal of peppers.

Squeak loved peppers because back in the day, all of them were extremely sweet. Squeak always ate sweet things, so his obsession with peppers was understandable. He had numerous miniature pepper plants popping out of his floor; tiny, bright, juicy pepper plants growing on his windowsills craning toward the sun; and peppers growing in his tiny garden. However, Squeak only grew miniature peppers that were "his size."

Squeak could be seen as a mouse who was rather timid, just as his image. Even though he was a medium-sized mouse, he was bashful and reserved. Besides his shyness, he was also silly and uncareful. Squeak was a young mouse who had just moved away

from his parents and family in order to adapt to the outside world around him. Because he had just moved away four months ago, he was clumsy and his hut was usually messy. However, after some time, he was able to get used to everything.

Squeak had a rather simple schedule, which he always kept to every day. All of his activities always somehow related to peppers. Suddenly, one day, while Squeak was brushing his teeth, a miraculous thing happened. He noticed a thin red pepper wiggling around on its stem on the windowsill all by itself! After some time, it finally broke free from its stem, falling into the bathtub. The red pepper rolled over, becoming chubby and thick all of a sudden.

Squeak shook his head; it just simply could not be happening! As he spat out the pepper toothpaste and water in his mouth, he cautiously reached out to pick the pepper up. The pepper rolled away, farther from his quivering outstretched paw, and suddenly stood up on its tip. Squeak shrank away in terror as the pepper wiggled again.

An angry face carved into the red pepper glared at Squeak. Squeak let out a shriek as the pepper hopped threateningly toward him. Squeak let out another squeak as more peppers, this time a green and yellow one, wiggled their way off of their stems and started toward Squeak. Fury and hatred written on their faces, they sprang toward Squeak, who immediately dashed out of the bathroom, slamming the door behind him.

Peppers rarely grew faces, and they only did when they felt extremely agitated. Their leader had been eaten the day before, and all of the peppers decided that it was time to take action. It would be rather hard to rule over themselves with their leader gone . . .

Sweat dripped down Squeak's furry and anxious face as he

locked the bathroom's door and stuffed cotton in all of the cracks in the door. Squeak promised to himself that the next day, he would build a new bathroom away from the old one, pepper-free.

The following day, while Squeak hurriedly built a new bathroom, the peppers inside the old one sighed sadly. Their friends and cousins were being eaten! They surely had to do something about it! Whispering and murmuring to each other quietly, they developed ideas that could possibly stop Squeak from eating them all. This then led to their magnificent and devious plan . . .

On the other hand, Squeak sighed and slumped down into his chair, thinking about what to do. The angry faces of the peppers popped into his mind once more, and then he decided he would have to go ask Dr. Hopper the cricket, the best doctor around, for help. Squeak immediately set off the next day to Dr. Hopper's office for advice.

"Hello, Squeak, how might I help you today?" Dr. Hopper asked pleasantly, as he casually leaned back into his chair.

Outside, Squeak could see an innocent-looking gopher hovering around the window, whistling and picking up trash outside. Squeak looked at him, waiting for him to leave, but he did not. Finally deciding that there was no point in waiting, he sat down timidly. Squeak nervously looked around, eyeing the potions and jars behind Dr. Hopper, glinting words on labels that said "Pig Pox Cure" and "Potion to make Blueberries Pink." Dr. Hopper was a specialist in anything anyone could think of.

Thinking that he would have nothing to lose, Squeak mumbled out his entire incident with the peppers. After explaining everything to Dr. Hopper, who seemed to be in deep thought, Squeak felt his

face burn red with embarrassment. He shifted in his seat and twiddled with his fingers as he waited for Dr. Hopper's reply.

"Well . . . " Dr. Hopper said after thinking for a long period of time,

"Now that I think about it, there *is* a way to get rid and stop those peppers."

"What is it?" Squeak begged, impatient to get an answer.

Dr. Hopper only smiled and got up from his seat, searching the shelves behind him for a potion. After a long time while Dr. Hopper was searching for a cure, knocking over bottles and small containers as he did so, Squeak felt rather let down, thinking that he would never be able to get rid of the peppers. However, just about when Squeak decided that there would be nothing to help him, Dr. Hopper muttered a small "Ah ha!" to himself as he held up a tiny purple bottle toward the light.

"Yes! Yes indeed! This is the very bottle!" Dr. Hopper said gleefully, setting the bottle down on his desk.

Squeak clapped his hands excitedly, grinning as he did so. Squeak examined the bottle carefully as Dr. Hopper went into a long explanation about how to use it.

"Now, inside this bottle is extremely powerful powder," said Dr. Hopper seriously, "and you must wear gloves while handling this. Once you get home, immediately sprinkle this over the pepper plants. This will make them go back to normal and not, well, be alive. Well, I mean, you can still eat them, but they won't attack you or become 'alive' when you eat them."

Squeak nodded and then gulped. He understood and guessed that the powder would be extremely pricey, but he was willing to do anything to stop the peppers from attacking him.

"How much is this?" Squeak whispered hoarsely to Dr. Hopper, who was twirling his mustache with one of his extremely long legs.

"Well, for you . . . it is free! I've never heard of such peppers and I am determined and eager to help you with this! If it does not work, you may return the powder and well, I'm afraid you will have to pull out every pepper plant in your home. You will also have to board up your bathroom because you may not know what may happen," Mr. Hopper exclaimed.

"Oh, well, I guess I might as well stop eating them. I haven't really liked them after that . . . incident. I will be leaving now. Thank you very, very much!" Squeak said happily.

Once Squeak got home, he rushed to the bathroom, bringing the powder with him. He slowly opened the door of the bathroom, nervous and anxious.

Boing! Boing! Boing! Boing! Many colorful peppers charged toward him, all with the same angry face. In a hurry, Squeak quickly shut the door.

Squeak shook and trembled with fear, sweating. After mustering as much courage as he could, he opened the door again. To his relief, all of the peppers were in the planter in the windowsill, looking completely normal. Quickly, Squeak showered the peppers with the white powder and stepped away. However, the thing he did not know was that the peppers had sent a messenger—the gopher that was near the window at Dr. Hopper's—to spy on him to see what he was doing.

Earlier, when the gopher told the peppers about Squeak's plan, all the peppers panicked. How were they going to save themselves?

As the peppers become more alarmed, the air began to burn and irritate the peppers, causing their skin to blister and turn red.

"What's happening?" one pepper howled.

Suddenly, a fly swooped into the bathroom and bit a pepper. However, while flying away, the fly screamed and dropped to the ground.

"I think you've suddenly become spicy!" the gopher said, surprised. "Quick! I think I know how you defeat Squeak!"

Since the gopher was a farmer, he was well known among the plants, fruits, and vegetables because of his special ability to chat with them. He talked with his plants a lot, asking them if they were doing well, and what they needed. This situation was just another like he'd seen millions of times while working in the field. The gopher had also created "medicine" for the plants. At this moment, he knew exactly what to do.

Quickly, the gopher and the peppers worked together to create a lotion from the peppers' sweat that made them immune to the powder Squeak had gotten.

Afterwards, Squeak sprinkled all of the peppers with powder. One pepper suddenly leapt up and bit him on the finger.

Squeak shrieked and slammed the door behind him, as all of the peppers sprang down from the windowsill. Squeak then quickly boarded up the door and threw out all of the remaining peppers in his house. He got rid of anything that was or related to peppers, and ended up liking carrots instead.

However, inside the boarded-up bathroom stood hundreds of peppers cheering and jumping up and down. Not only did they stop Squeak from eating their kind but they also kept them safe from any other predators! From that day on, the peppers handed down the lotion to younger generations to protect them in the future from others like Squeak. It made them taste extremely spicy and hot.

The peppers from the Battle of Squeak promised their descendants a long life with the magnificent lotion they created. Because they took a stand, to this day, present-day peppers remain as spicy and as fiery as they did long ago.

Heart of the Poem

Polly Alice McCann helped Lila Tierney determine how to make readers feel what she's feeling in her poem, "Treasures."

Dear Reader,

My happy job is to help you think about revision of your poem. I want to ask you some questions about your poem. The questions will help you decide if there are any changes you'd like to make after you've written it. Usually, you'll find one or two things you'd like to change. Sometimes people change lots of things, or none at all.

One thing I like about poetry: I like to think about how it looks on the page. Another thing I do—I reread it and pretend I am another person who has never seen the poem. Then I decide if I've really said everything I wanted to say. Sometimes I call this the heart of the poem. All that means is that I wonder if I truly and really do say what I absolutely mean to say. I ask myself questions like: Does my poem help the reader imagine the same things I'm imagining? Does the reader feel the same things I'm feeling?

Those answers often make me add a few words or change a word picture. Sometimes I move the words around to new places because I think one is a special surprise and I want them in just the right order for my reader to get the most enjoyment out of them.

Rhyme: If it doesn't rhyme, that is okay. If it rhymes, great! Sometimes a poet will pick a word that doesn't quite rhyme enough because it fits the heart of the poem better. But I see that this poem is ABCB pattern. That does give it the feel of the rhythm of walking. If rhyming is super important and sometimes it is for me too, try this website: *http://wikirhymer.com/* It has near rhymes, which allow for more choices!

Here are some things to try on a poem:

- Try reading your poem without the last line in each stanza. What is the heart of the poem now?
- Try reading without the third line in each stanza. What happens to the poem's meaning then?
- If you find a line that doesn't match the heart of the poem, or what you really meant to say, think about a way to fix that and try out some new words there instead. Try on three or four words or phrases until you pick your favorite for that

stanza. It's like trying on clothes.

- Look at the third line in each stanza again. What words to you see? What can you do to make that stand out even more?
- Check each word, even each "and" and "a"–Do you want them all there? Do you need them all there?
- Finished? Your poem is ready to go!!

Sincerely,
Polly Alice McCann

Polly Alice McCann, poet and artist, writes children's books. She thinks writing is about remembering what is worth saving for the future. She loves to grow basil and explore new adventures with her family and friends. She has an enormous coonhound dog and two kids. She lives near a stream with a bridge north of Kansas City, Missouri. Find her at *newthingartstudio.com*.

Lila Tierney

Lila spends half the year in Portland, Oregon and the other in Lafayette, Louisiana—so she enjoys both Chapman Elementary and homeschool, where she just completed third grade. At age four, Lila fell in love with *The Tree That Time Built*, poems inspired by nature. The rhyme and musicality of poetry appeals to her. Soon she composed her own. What inspires her? Nature, humor, history, and simpler times. Lila carries a sketchbook everywhere and is crazy about reading. Her favorite poetry book is *Suzie Bitner Was Afraid of the Drain* by Barbara Vance. When she's not writing poetry, she likes to perform on stage as a pianist, ballerina, or actor. She plays soccer (and the penny whistle), practices Aikido, and loves art. In the future, she wants to be a forest ecologist and teach others about nature through poems, stories, and children's book illustrations.

Polly Alice McCann: When did you first begin writing poetry? What made you start?

Lila Tierney: I don't know. I just did. Probably when I was four or five. I have a little book I write them in. I really like Shel Silverstein and *Suzie Bitner Was Afraid of the Drain* and "Don't Bunk the Glunk."

Q: What do you like best about your poem that's going to be published? What do you think is the heart of your poem?

A: I like the last line in each stanza the best. I like how each line is fast

. . . and about how the adults don't pay attention but kids do.

Q: Why did you think to put a "waxy chestnut" reference in your poem?
A: They grow here! I collect them and use them when I build little fairy houses in the back yard. And when we had to get ready to go away for the summer, my mom helped me collect them into a jar to put in my window.

Q: I like that about your poem, all those parts of the poem that are nuanced like reflections—the reflection on the chestnut and then on the window. Why did you revise that part of your poem then?
A: I didn't like that stanza of the poem. I didn't think "voices on the radio" worked. I like it better now.

Q: But what about when you are not writing poetry, what do you do then?
A: I like to play the piano, dance, play soccer—and I taught myself the penny whistle!

Treasures

by
Lila Tierney

I found a penny on the pavement–
have to check the date.
Mama rushes me along,
we are late late late.

I found a little piece of string.
It could hold a fairy swing.
A man beeps his horn
and hears his phone ring.

I found a muddy acorn cap
it holds soup or salad nicely.
A woman types a note
and checks the time precisely.

I found a stick with bug writing,
shaped like a fairy chair.
Teacher shushes all the students
and aims a fiery stare.

I found a smooth and waxy chestnut
to add to my collection.
A cyclist speeds by a storefront
and checks out his reflection.

I found a green translucent button.
It's a window to the world.
A man bumps his elbow
and out his coffee swirled.

While grown-ups go about
their daily tasks and feats,
little girls go out to seek and find
the treasures of the streets.

Twists and Turns

Dear Reader,

Saketh's story, "Sean's Adventure to Ancient Egypt," is well developed with an enticing beginning and a satisfying ending. What stood out to me the most were the surprising twists and turns in the story. Writers who add twists and turns in their story keep their readers intrigued and wondering what's going to happen next.

Have you ever read a story you just couldn't put down? Chances are it was full of surprising twists! So how do writers come up with twists? Saketh took inspiration from objects surrounding him. The green ball that appears in the beginning of his story was actually his favorite green ball lying on the floor in his bedroom while he wrote the story.

If you're trying to infuse your story with a surprising twist, ask yourself, what could be the worst thing that could happen to your character right now? If your character hates spiders, why not have one fall onto his shoulder in the middle of class? Another strategy is to take a walk outside. A change of scenery will often allow your thoughts to drift. Walking and thinking can be more motivating than sitting and thinking.

Enjoy the adventure!
Jena Brigantino

Jena Brigantino grew up playing outdoors in central California, where she dreamed up stories featuring animals. Jena wishes she had the opportunity to experience an Inklings program as a child. She strives to extend the opportunity to as many children as possible as Managing Director of Society of Young Inklings. She holds a BA in creative arts and a minor in education from San José State University.

Saketh Elumalai

Saketh was born on March 15, 2010 in California. His native country is India but he is also an American citizen. His hobbies are reading, playing, watching TV, drawing, coloring, doing word searches, and crossword puzzles. His favorite subjects are math, English, and art. He also likes to roller skate and ice skate. He is in first grade at James Leitch Elementary School. His favorite sports are dodgeball, football, basketball, badminton, and soccer. He is also a huge Harry Potter fan.

Jena Brigantino: When did you start writing?

Saketh Elumalai: I started writing when my mom asked me, "Saketh, do you want to write a story?" I was five years old back then. My first story was called "The Wise Owls and the Cruel Witch." Before this, I liked writing essays on different topics. When everybody appreciated me, I wanted to write more stories.

Q: Where do you like to write?

A: I like to write in my bedroom because I get ideas from my toys, library books, and games. I also get ideas from the posters and stickers in my room.

Q: How do you come up with your ideas?

A: I read a lot of books. Books help me imagine lots of things. Also I think about what happens around me. I like to write about things that are not possible in reality because anything can be possible in a story.

Q: How do you feel about the revision you made in your story?
A: I feel very good about my revision process because it made my story perfect. The revision I did with my mentor helped me write a great twist in my story.

Q: What advice do you have for other Inklings who don't like revision very much?
A: My advice is, "Guys, revision is very important to authors and it makes your story even more stronger." I strongly recommend that you revise because you might get more interesting ideas.

Sean's Adventure to Ancient Egypt

by

Saketh Elumalai

Chapter One: The Glowing Ball

Once upon a time, there was a boy called Sean. He was seven years old, four feet tall, and liked wearing green T-shirts. He lived in Groundhog Common, California. His room had fifty-five toys, lots of books, and a door. His room looked packed and had one big window. Sean had lots of green balls. And, amongst his green balls, the bouncy bright green ball was his favorite one.

One Tuesday, while Sean was eating lunch in his room, he suddenly got startled by a ball that was rolling towards him. He accidentally tipped his glass of water on the ball. And guess what? It happened to be his favorite bright green ball!

Immediately, the ball shot green light, which reflected on his window. Sean watched it with amazement and he noticed a green portal, which had opened to the size of a big book. Sean had a feeling that he wanted to step inside the portal. So, he grabbed his backpack

and filled it with books, food, a flashlight and a water bottle.

Then he nervously marched directly into the portal.

Chapter Two: The Tickling Portal

Once Sean stepped inside the portal, he felt as though he was being tickled. Sean started to laugh, but he couldn't hear anything. The trip in the portal lasted for a few minutes.

When he finally stepped out, Sean looked around eagerly. He saw pyramids, a mummy's tomb, the Sphinx, and also met a group of people. The people were dressed with animal skin. Sean realized that he landed in ancient Egypt and the people were ancient Egyptians.

Sean was nervous, but he was determined to speak to the people. Then Sean talked to them, and found out that he was in the city of Maya. Maya was one of the many cities in ancient Egypt, just like Fremont is one of the cities in California.

Chapter Three: Sean's Helpful Nature

As Sean continued his journey in the city of Maya, he met another group of people and the leader of the group told Sean that he and his people were all Mayans.

The Mayans looked very frightened, so Sean asked the people, "Why do you all look so worried?"

One of the Mayans told Sean that they were frightened by a huge monster, which was fierce, fat, tall and scary-looking. Another person mentioned that the monster troubled the Mayans by darting at them when the people went up the hill to fetch fruits for the group to eat. Another person told Sean they were starving because they could not go past the monster. Sean really wanted to rescue the Mayans from the monster.

Sean told the Mayans, "Please do not be frightened and I will find a way to fight the monster."

So, Sean set out to find the monster. After what seemed like an hour, Sean saw a huge monster walking towards him. By the shape of the monster, Sean realized that the monster was not a monster at all. It was actually an Ankylosaur. However, it looked just like the Mayans had described to him.

The Ankylosaur had started running towards Sean because he was wearing an attractive green T-shirt, as the dinosaur's favorite color was green. Sean thought the Ankylosaur was trying to attack him with its clubbed tail, and so he quickly started running very fast. Unknowingly, he ran into an empty room. It was a dimly lit room.

Chapter Four: 1003-Year-Old Master Kwan and His Students

The dimly lit room was getting its light from one candle placed on a stand in the middle of the room. The room looked ancient and had scary-looking corners. The room didn't have mechanical things. It only had an enormous mat. Sean sat on the mat and waited for somebody to come in. After waiting till night, he got bored and started reading one of his books from his backpack and slowly fell asleep.

The next morning, the door opened and in came a very old man with ten children. They looked at Sean, who was sleeping, and wondered, *Who is this boy?* The children bravely tried to wake him up

and Sean got up. He got startled by looking at the surprised children and the old man.

The old man approached Sean and introduced himself by saying, "Hello, my name is Kwan and I am a karate teacher. This is my classroom and I am 1003 years old. You can call me Master Kwan."

Next, he asked Sean where he came from. Sean then explained to him about the portal, his meeting with the Mayans, his thought of rescuing the Mayans and finally about the chasing Ankylosaur. Master Kwan and the children carefully listened to what Sean said.

Then, the master offered to help Sean.

Chapter Five: Master Kwan's Special Power

"Since I am a very old karate teacher, you can learn karate with me so that you can fight the Ankylosaur" said Master Kwan. Even though Sean was nervous, he was determined to learn and help the Mayans.

Master Kwan had a special power preserved for a very special person. He thought Sean was a special person because he travelled from the present world to the ancient world through a portal. He also thought Sean had a very kind heart because he wanted to rescue the Mayans whom he had never met before.

His special power was to learn all karate moves very quickly. The power was stored in an object, which looked like a small green planet. Master Kwan twisted the object and let the power flow into Sean's mind. He felt very powerful after this process.

Then began the advanced karate lessons between Master Kwan and Sean.

Chapter Six: The Battle between the Karate Kids and the Ankylosaur

With his special power, Sean learnt all the karate moves in a short period of time. After Sean passed the advanced karate lessons, he was ready to face the dinosaur. Sean and the children set out to the same hill where he first saw the Ankylosaur.

The children found the animal and they battled under Sean's leadership. Sean was using his tricky karate moves, which were very quick for the dinosaur to react. Sean and the children were being very intelligent. At last, Sean and the children won the battle and the Ankylosaur accepted his defeat.

The animal then said, "I will not continue to do the bad deeds to the Mayans anymore."

The Mayans were watching the whole war from the bottom of the hill. They felt very glad that the Ankylosaur was defeated and they were very pleased with Sean.

The Mayans kneeled before Sean as they all thanked him.

Chapter Seven: The Little Seed

After accomplishing his task, Sean decided to get back to his home. Sean went back to the pyramids to find the portal. But the portal was gone! He was worried because he didn't know how to get back to his home without the portal.

He went to Master Kwan and explained to him his problem. Master Kwan looked very worried. Master Kwan thought of a way to

help Sean, and he went into his classroom and walked out with a little seed.

He gave it to Sean and said, "Drop this seed where the portal first opened near the pyramids, and the same portal will open again."

Sean thanked Master Kwan and went back to the pyramids. Sean followed Master Kwan's instruction and the portal opened again.

Sean said goodbye to his friends who were all gathered around him. The Mayans happily wished Sean farewell.

Now, he once again nervously stepped inside the tickling portal . . .

THE END

Moral: Never give up on helping others.

Conflict

Dear Reader,

Tiffanie did something very brave in this piece of writing. She changed her first draft almost completely. Sometimes as writers we have to admit when a first idea exists only as a way to bring us to what a story is meant to be. This is very much what happened with Tiffanie's story.

In the first draft, she had an incredibly compelling voice and character but she needed to zero in on the conflict for her character. She needed to figure out where he was, what he wanted, and what was in the way of what he wanted. In that first draft, she gave her reader some beautiful, specific details right away (the "hushed chorus of ten thousand voices"), but the story left me with several questions she hadn't answered. Still, these questions let us discuss where this piece needed to go in the next draft. The most important question was: what will be the driving conflict for this story?

Her first draft felt dreamy and ephemeral with the main character attempting to remember something that mattered to him,
so my question to Tiffanie was: what is he trying to remember
and why is he having such a hard time doing it? Throughout
our first discussion, it was clear that Tiffanie needed to flesh out
the answer to this question before the central conflict would be
clear for the reader. This is a normal discovery process as a writer and very much part of the natural revision process; however,
often writers have trouble letting go of their words in order to
take a story to the next level.

Not Tiffanie. She turned in a wholly transformed second draft!
She took our discussion to heart and rewrote her piece to present a clear character, setting, and conflict. The story came together and leapt off the page! I applaud how willing Tiffanie
was to throw out so much of her first draft, to dig into the core
of what she was writing and find the specific conflict that would
drive the next draft forward. In that first draft, she had created potential for a rich, captivating story, but the story ended
up working because she took the feedback and applied it so
fiercely to her drafting process.

Tiffanie proved in this process that writing is truly rewriting!

Happy drafting,
Kim Culbertson

Kim Culbertson is the award-winning author of the YA
novels *Songs for a Teenage Nomad* (Sourcebooks 2010), *Instructions
for a Broken Heart* (Sourcebooks 2011), *Catch a Falling Star* (Scholastic
2014), *The Possibility of Now* (Scholastic 2016), and *The Wonder of Us*
(Scholastic 2017). Much of her inspiration for her novels comes from
the work she's done as a high school teacher since 1997. In 2012,
Kim wrote her eBook novella *The Liberation of Max McTrue* for her
students, who, over the years, have taught her far more than she
has taught them. She is a member of SCBWI, Sierra Writers, and the
National Writing Project Writers Council. She currently lives in Nevada
City, California, with her husband and daughter.

Tiffanie Huang

Eighth grader Tiffanie is passionate about writing both novels and shorter pieces of fiction, including poetry and flash fiction. Recently, she won a Silver Medal award at the national level and several Gold Key awards at the regional level of the 2017 Scholastic Art & Writing Awards contest. Tiffanie was also selected to be published in the Spring 2017 *Poetic Power Anthology* and was a semifinalist in the 2016 *Lascaux Review*. She has had her own share of music award ceremonies, though none as prestigious as the one from "Music Lessons." Besides writing, she plays the piano and cello.

Kim Culbertson: What was your biggest challenge when redrafting this story?

Tiffanie Huang: The most difficult part of the editing process was thinking of an ending that wrapped up the story neatly and smoothly. I also ended up tweaking the entire story, with the exception of the first paragraph!

Q: How did focusing on conflict elevate the overall impact of the story?

A: When my mentor mentioned the conflict, I realized the piece needed more action and less thinking. This sped up the story and made it much more refreshing to read.

Q: What is the relationship between conflict and character for you as a writer?

A: For me, conflict isn't just what slides in between characters and what keeps it moving. I like to think of conflict as a whole new character interfering with other people in the story.

Q: Where do you find your inspiration for a story?

A: As a musician, I have been invited to similar award ceremonies (though none with as much talk from the president of the board) and it occurred to me that I have never seen a person with a disability play before. I found this ironic given the fact that one of the greatest classical composers, Ludwig van Beethoven, was deaf towards the end of his career. Louis Braille, credited with the invention of the braille alphabet for blind people, happened to be an accomplished cellist and organist.

Q: What are you most proud of in this process?

A: I was glad that I could find a way to describe the main character's surroundings without the advantage of sight. In addition, I'm proud of being able to scrap 90% of my story so that I could improve. Looking back, I think the sacrifice definitely paid off.

Music Lessons

by

Tiffanie Huang

As soon as I enter, the whispers begin. A hushed chorus of ten thousand voices rasping softly. In my mind, I can see cupped hands and stolen glances, nervous titters from the shadows. I can feel the eyes drawn to me from every corner of the auditorium, from every person in the room.

My assistant inches me to the piano, step by step, and for a moment, I am worried that impatience would radiate from the audience. I swallow down the tangle of anxiety and turn to face the audience.

I clear my throat awkwardly and wet my lips: "I am very honored to be here today and performing for all of you."

Somewhere in a nook in the back of my mind, a voice incredibly like my former piano teacher's pinches at me.

They're not listening to you. They're watching. They're waiting for you to make a mistake.

My voice is hoarse as I continue. "It is a pleasure for me to be

able to tell you my story through music. I hope you enjoy." I dip my head like I'd practiced so many times.

The piano bench groans under my weight as I hurry to adjust it. Sweat glosses my palms, but it all feels cold, even in the heat of the stage lights. As I smooth them out on my dress pants, there seems to be a tingle of anxiety in the air. With my feet, I search for the piano pedals and check to make sure they are in working condition.

Because you're blind, you have no chance. Your standards are lower, your opportunities are fewer.

A stray arrow of nostalgia strikes me immediately after my fingers sweep past the first three notes. I silently hope that I am not the klutz my teacher told me I was at every lesson. I send a desperate prayer that she was mistaken, that I could grow to become a pianist.

I can still feel her biting words cutting through my skin, shredding any little fragments of confidence I had left into black-and-white confetti.

Honey, there's no way you can be a professional with those eyes of yours. I don't want you to get your hopes up. You shouldn't even be thinking about it. You can't even find the right keys to press . . .

I shake her words from my mind and play. The rush of the piece is exhilarating, and soon its energy consumes me. I find myself lost in the intricately woven passages and the hidden lyrics underneath the blanket of technique and rhythms. The melody is hypnotizing and lulling at the same time, and I feel static electricity through my whole body.

Prove them wrong. Prove her wrong. Show them you are capable of doing something.

As I draw myself out of the flurry of keys, I do not end with a final flourish, like most pianists do. I end with one single note—one single note that remains ringing even as I release my hands.

The silence is deafening. But in that moment, I realize how much more of an impact this lone note had than a series of enormous chords.

The stillness is welcoming. Not a single auditorium chair squeaks.

I stand up and bow, and I am greeted with thunderous applause, a rainstorm of relief after a long drought of self-doubt.

My assistant arrives and helps me get backstage. She straightens my tie and guides me along with two other young composers to the stage again for the award ceremony.

The International Young Composers' Competition president shakes all of us by the hand and hands each of us a certificate and plaque. I feel the vibrations of his heavy footsteps as he walks to the podium to deliver his speech. Everything whooshes by so quickly that I do not absorb everything he says. I do, however, remember him speaking about why we were the composers chosen for this honor.

" . . . This young man here—" He's able to place a hand on my shoulder since I am sitting closest. "—was selected as one of the three honorees because of how touching his piece was. He was not given the award *despite* being blind; rather, it might have even been of use. Our composer here brought emotion into the music instead of simply planting what he saw into music." The president then concludes with a polite plea for donations in order to support the composing foundation.

With the help of my walking stick, I exit the auditorium. Behind me, a prim, weathered voice catches my attention.

"Excuse me," says the woman, who is probably in her sixties by the sound of it. "I really wanted to tell you how that piece warmed my heart, but I can't put it into words."

I turn towards her. The air outside is blissfully cool and my fears abandon me.

I try to smile at her, but there's something off about the way she's talking, the way she sounds, the way she feels.

"I do hope you still remember your piano teacher from five years ago," she hints, unaware of the ice crystallizing throughout my body. My lips are numb and refuse to open.

When I do not speak, she continues cheerfully. "I'm so glad to see you becoming a budding pianist and achieving your dreams. Look at us! Look at how hard work pays off! Perhaps we will have the opportunity to work together again?"

I realize she is inviting me to join her studio again with the convenient timing of my award ceremony. And with that bit of magic, my lips instantly find their will to un-numb.

"I appreciate your compliment, but I think I learned everything you had to teach me. Thank you."

As I beat a hasty retreat to the silver Prius waiting faithfully for me in the parking lot, I discover my newfound appreciation for being unable to see. Still, I imagine her indignant expression and it makes me smile a little.

Character Motivation

Loraine McCormick and Louisa Phlaum worked together on what motivates the hero in Louisa's story, "In the Depths of the Pool."

Dear Reader,

Louisa's Pflaum's story, "In the Depths of the Pool," is an imaginative tale of fairies, their unique world, and a character named Grace who is determined to reach her life's goal. Most of the fairies are sweet and kind and have welcomed little Grace into their world. Grace, even though she is as small as a fairy, endures exclusion because she is not a "real fairy."

I noticed an opportunity for Louisa to highlight Grace's determination, so I chose character motivation as our revision focus. Character motivation is what drives the hero on a daily basis. There is external motivation—the character is determined to achieve some physical reward like a trophy, money, a lost or stolen item, etc. There is also internal motivation—the character is motivated by an inner desire like knowledge, pride, overcoming fear, etc. In literature, characters usually have a motivation behind every action or behavior. Motivations lead to action, and action leads to more action. And problems. And conflict. And problems and conflicts create great stories.

In Louisa's original version, she shows how much Grace loved the pool and the synchronized swimming sport of Bankmant—one of many new words that Louisa created. Through our character motivation focus, Louisa rewrote sections that now highlight Grace's external and internal motivations. Grace's external motivation—her life goal—is to be a Bankmant performer. Her internal motivation—her heart's desire—is to receive unconditional acceptance from the fairies, who are Grace's only family now. Grace will never forget her mother's final words: "Believe in yourself." These words drive Grace toward her goal.

Louisa beautifully revised the narrative and dialogue to show Grace's struggles and her laser-focus motivation to be accepted as a Bankmant performer. Grace's frustration grows as the story progresses, and her motivation intensifies each time the fairies deny her. The story is now more exciting, and the reader can cheer Grace on to overcome obstacles as she tries to prove to the fairies that she is worthy of performing, even if she is not a "real fairy." Grace tries to convince them that her skills, not her heritage, should be the most important consideration. Louisa created a richer story by developing and emphasizing what was already there. Grace's motivation and her internal journey are now clearer. It almost always strengthens a story when we make things more difficult for our characters.

In addition to expanding the character motivation, Louisa worked more on the villain in the story. Even within this seemingly idyllic fairy world, something sinister lurks in the shadows. Louisa wove in something unexpected that threatens to undermine all of Grace's hard work to achieve her goal. I love the way that Louisa shows Grace developing into a confident character who is determined to reach her goal against all the odds.

When you are writing your story, ask yourself: What does your main character want more than anything in the world? What are they trying to achieve? Once you know what your character's goal is, then you can begin imagining all the possible scenarios and the actions the character will have to take to reach their goal, which includes the presence of some type of conflict that tries to counteract every action your main character takes throughout the story.

I hope that you'll enjoy "In the Depths of the Pool" as much as I did.

Happy writing!
Loraine McCormick

Loraine McCormick teaches creative writing through the Society of Young Inklings, and she edits children's books. She is a member of the Society of Children's Book Writers and Illustrators. She has a BA in advertising, with a concentration in English, from San José State University. She's worked as a copywriter and as a technical editor. Currently, she is writing several children's picture books, as well as a middle-grade novel. She's raised two sons and lives in San José, California, with her husband and a goldendoodle named Ginger.

Louisa Pflaum

Louisa is nine years old and lives in Portola Valley, California. She really likes sushi, but never the wasabi. Her favorite subjects in school are social studies, science, and art. Louisa's family owns a pet dog named Wilbur.

Loraine McCormick: What gave you the idea to write "In the Depths of the Pool"?

Louisa Pflaum: I got the idea from my teacher at school. We were in our fantasy unit, and we were supposed to write an adapted fairy tale. That gave me an idea for my book. I wanted to write a longer fantasy that others could adapt from.

Q: When did you start writing stories?

A: I started writing stories in late first grade. At first I wasn't that interested, but then (in third grade), I started to do Society of Young Inklings, and it was an opportunity for me to freely write.

Q: Are you working on a new story?

A: I started to write a new story, but then I thought I should focus more on "In the Depths of the Pool." Plus, I wasn't enjoying my new story.

Q: Our revision focus was character motivation. What does that mean to you?

A: It meant that we wanted Grace to really desire her goal, destiny. I liked that because I only mentioned Bankmant once or twice, and it doesn't seem like she really wanted it.

Q: What changed in the story when you revised or added character motivation elements?

A: I felt like my story became broader when we started working on character motivation because it seems like Grace really desires Bankmant.

Q: Do you like your story now that it has been revised?

A: I like it much more than before because we added in some key details.

Q: How did you like the revision process?

A: I really enjoyed the revision process. I got the opportunity to work with another writer who has more experience than I do and saw my story from a different point of view.

Q: What advice would you give other writers about revision?

A: The advice I would give other writers is to not think that if you are revising that it means your story is bad. It just means you want your story to be the best it can be.

In the Depths of
the Pool

by

Louisa Pflaum

Chapter One: Rescued by Fairies

Grace Kingston was eleven years old. But she didn't know that. Why? That's what I'm about to tell you. When Grace was just two, her parents died in a fire.

It was a peaceful night. Two happy parents were playing by the warm fireplace with their toddler, Grace. Suddenly, a spark flew through the fireplace screen. The spark caught on the rug. The rug burst into flames. The fire spread onto anything it could get to. The chimney collapsed, trapping her parents behind a pile of bricks. All Grace could remember was her mom whispering to her, "Believe in yourself."

Then, Grace saw a creature with wings hovering above her. The creature seemed to have an evil twinkle in his eye. But, luckily for Grace, a large group of fairies rescued little Grace in the nick of time.

Ever since then, the fairies took care of her. Grace considered

the fairies her many parents. Grace had always been an unusual child. Ever since she was born, she had been as small as an apple. That is why she fit in so well with the fairies—except when it came to Bankmant.

In this small and magical fairy world, there was a very popular sport called Bankmant, where a group of four would make a synchronized routine in the pool. A panel of five judges decided which team did the best.

Grace felt the fairies were always edging her out when she said how much she wanted to play. It was her dream, her passion. But the fairies always found ways to let her down. Even the nicest fairies. They were polite about it, but Grace could always tell what they were actually saying: *"Bankmant is only for the true fairies."* And sometimes Grace actually led herself to believe them. What if Bankmant *is* only for fairies? But even at those times, a chunk of her heart always felt like it was missing. And Grace knew a part, that part of her heart, was meant for Bankmant.

Chapter Two: The Storm

One sunny day, Grace was helping a fairy named Anne trim the bushes in the garden. She was thinking about a Bankmant routine that she had seen a group of fairies perform at the last Bankmank show. Suddenly, there was a thundering noise from overhead. Anne instantly looked up.

"Grace! Get inside! A storm is coming!"

Suddenly, the rain pelted down like needles into the ground. As Grace raced back to her apartment, she hollered over the deafening noise.

"But what about you!?" Grace screamed.

"Don't worry about me. I'm going to warn the others!" yelled Anne.

To you, rain and wind are probably just little things, but to fairies, they can be very, very, deadly because rain droplets are enormous when you're only as tall as an apple.

Seven minutes later, the fairies were safe inside their homes. Grace decided to read. Almost all of the books she owned were about Bankmant. She chose her favorite book, *How to Win at Bankmant*, but she was distracted by the storm. She was constantly looking out the window. Something about that storm gave her a bad, bad, feeling. So bad that she soon had a terrible headache. There was something about this storm. Something that seemed familiar. This was no ordinary storm. The weather was usually never like this!

Later, when Grace tried again to read her Bankmant book, something outside caught her eye. A dark figure was looming toward the door. As the figure got closer, Grace's heart started beating harder and faster. The doorknob rattled and in walked Anne. Grace let out a sigh of relief.

"Oh, Anne! You scared me!" cried Grace.

"Oh, sorry!" replied Anne. "I didn't mean to!"

Just then, Grace realized that Anne was drenched from head to toe.

"You must be freezing! Let me get you something to eat. Would you like a brownie?"

"Why, thank you, Grace! How thoughtful of you! Yes, please, a brownie would be nice!"

As Anne bit into the ooey, gooey chocolate brownie, she said, "Grace, baking is your destiny, not Bankmant. Don't go chasing after something that you know you'll never get to."

Grace grunted. Anne placed her warm but rough hand on Grace's hand.

Trying to ignore Anne's comment, Grace exploded with questions. "How did it go? How wet was it? Was anybody hurt?"

Anne laughed. "It was fine. No one was hurt, although some cocoa trees fell down." Grace breathed a sigh of relief. Everything was all right. Or so she thought.

Chapter Three: The Pool

That night, Grace lay awake in her bed for what seemed like forever. Finally, she fell asleep. Grace heard a knock on the door.

"Come in!" Grace responded groggily.

It was Anne. "Hi! Would you like to show all the fairies your amazing Bankmant moves?"

Grace couldn't believe her ears. "Sure!" Two minutes later, she was in the Bankmant stadium. All the fairies were watching her. Grace opened her eyes. Darn. She had been dreaming.

Suddenly, she heard a noise. Pat, pat, pat.

"It's just the rain. It's just the rain," Grace whispered to herself over and over again.

Even in her cozy apartment, she felt so uncomfortable. Then it hit her. What if a Biforam had created this terrible storm? The Biforams were another group of fairies. According to the fairies who Grace lived with, the Biforams were evil. They had powers to do things that no other living creature could do. And they definitely did not use those powers for good, but for evil. The Biforams were enemies of the fairies. Nobody quite knew why, though. Fairies weren't usually known for being mad at certain groups of other creatures.

In the morning, the rain stopped. The sun was just peeking from behind the clouds to start the day. Grace had always loved mornings! As she hummed a fairy tune, she made herself some eggs. When Grace finished her breakfast, she went outside. She had planned on going to the pool that morning, so she headed to the elevator. As the elevator slowly came, Grace thought about how glad she was that she had the pool! She absolutely loved the pool! It meant almost everything to her. She could spend time practicing her own Bankmant routines that she made up.

Grace lived in a mini apartment that was part of a giant building full of houses that all the fairies lived in. Each house had a bed, sofa, stove, and a bathroom, but, on the top floor of this great big building, there was a pool, spa, restaurant, and a game room. Whenever Grace had free time, she would hang out up there and watch the other fairies do their routines so she could practice perfecting her twirls and flips.

In one arm, Grace had a backpack with a book, glasses for reading, her towel, and her goggles. As the elevator reached floor 424, Grace hopped out. She went to the front desk, signed in, and grabbed a perfectly red apple. It was a special kind of apple. The kind that was small enough for Grace to be able to eat. Grace spotted a poster. It was a Bankmant poster. There was a Bankmant competition tonight! Grace headed over to the pool area.

You are probably thinking, how do fairies swim? And is it okay for their wings to get wet? Well, actually, most of the fairies cannot fly.

I don't know what those fairy tale books told you, but what I do know is that they did not tell you the truth! In Grace's group of fairies, only a few could fly. Unfortunately, though, all of the Biforams could fly.

In the case of the fairies who could fly, before hopping into the pool, they put a special gel on their wings that protected their wings and prevented them from getting wet. The fairies had special rules. If a fairy did something very good, like saving another fairy, they "earned" their wings. That way, the fairies didn't argue about who had wings and why.

Grace unpacked her towel and goggles. She put on her blue and yellow goggles. Immediately, she disappeared into the depths of the pool. On the opposite side of the pool was a group of fairies. They were very clearly a Bankmant team. Grace carefully watched their every move as they performed flips and twirls. That's what she did every day. Then, she heard a voice.

"What're you lookin' at, non-fairy?" snarled Alexandra.

Alexandra was often very rude. She was always the one who would tell Grace in the meanest way that she would never be a Bankmant performer.

"I may not be a real fairy, but at least I can do a triple flip," said Grace. Alexandra looked like her face was about to explode.

Chapter Four: Chores

Grace wrapped up her things and headed back to her mini apartment. Afterward, she headed toward the pond. It was time for her to do her chores.

Each fairy (including Grace) was required to perform three

chores every day, which is how they managed everyone living there. Grace's three chores were:

- Dinner Kitchen Committee. Grace was in charge of dessert. She always had a new surprise for the fairies.

- Berry Gatherer. Grace picked all of the perfectly ripe berries in the garden. Then she delivered them to the fairies who had signed up for berry deliveries.

- Water Gatherer. Grace went to the pond, pulling a wagon with five pails. She filled each pail, one by one, with water and then placed them in the wagon. Once Grace filled each and every one of the buckets up to the top, she took them to the kitchen on floor 424.

When Grace arrived at the pond, she filled the pails with water and then headed back to the kitchen. Grace knocked gently on the kitchen door, and Anne opened it.

"Hi there, Grace. Thank you for getting the water."

"You're welcome."

Anne let her inside, and Grace placed the buckets of water on the countertop. She grabbed two baskets, placed them in her wagon, and headed to the garden. Leah, the fairy, was already there. Her job was to grow the plants.

"Good morning, Leah," said Grace.

"Good morning, Grace. Ready for another day?"

"Yup, sure am," responded Grace cheerfully.

Grace let herself in through the gate and headed over to the cherry bush. She looked all over the bush for ripe berries. Part of the bush was dead. Something in the sky caught Grace's eye. She jerked around to get a better look.

"Leah, come look at this!"

"Oh my gosh! What happened? Wait . . . Oh no. Oh no, no, no!"

"What?" Grace asked eagerly.

"No ordinary fairy could have done this. It must have been . . . a Biforam," whispered Leah.

"I saw something just now. A hooded figure flying away," said Grace.

"No, that's the most terrible Biforam," said Leah. "That's Jacob Biforam."

Grace gasped.

Chapter Five: The Show

At 4:30 p.m., Grace headed back to the kitchen to prepare her dessert. She had decided to make chocolate lava cake. Grace was still shaken by her encounter with Jacob, but baking would calm her nerves. She was positive that her lava cake would be a complete hit. Grace let herself into the kitchen. She said hello to the rest of the dinner committee and headed to the dessert corner. Chloe, her partner for dessert, was already there.

"Hey, Grace. What are we going to make today?"

"Hi. I was thinking chocolate lava cake."

A dreamy look appeared in Chloe's eyes. She was known for loving chocolate. They got out the ingredients and got started. In two hours, they had baked 21,100 lava cakes!

Bzz! Bzz! A minute later, two fairies named Ella and Caroline zoomed into the room. They were two of the few fairies who could fly.

They were the ones who brought the food to the rest of the fairies. But another talent they had was delivering the food incredibly fast. Imagine delivering 21,100 lava cakes to the fairies while flying as fast as a bird!

As Grace started cleaning up, something caught her eye. It was another Bankmant poster. It read: "Bankmant show tonight at 8:30 p.m." She was again reminded about the Bankmant competition.

"I could never forget about a Bankmant competition," Grace thought.

Immediately, Grace raced over to the room where the fairies ate, had a quick meal, half of a lava cake, and rushed home. In Grace's little apartment, she took off her apron and jeans and put on her silk dress. Ten minutes later, Grace was in the swimming center. As Grace was finding a seat, she heard a voice.

"Grace! Oh my gosh, I've been looking all over for you!" It was Anne.

"Yes?" Grace replied, a little confused.

"Could you help me find a fairy to fill in for Katherine on the Golden Stars team? She's sick." This was Grace's chance.

Chapter Six: Let the Games Begin

"But Anne! I know their routine! At the pool—I've watched them for months!"

Anne hesitated. "Well, I mean, Bankmant is for true fairies…"

"Anne, why does that matter? I do everything the fairies do. Why must you exclude me from this?"

" . . . but . . . I'm sure we can make it work," Anne continued.

Grace beamed. This was a dream come true! Immediately, Grace raced over to the locker rooms to meet the Golden Stars team for the performance. As soon as she had learned their names, they got straight to work. The routine was super difficult! It had all sorts of flips and twirls. She kept telling herself, *"You always nail this at the pool. Do that now!"* Now all she needed to do was put on the team swimsuit that matched the others. The suit was dark gray with a golden star on the front. It shined even in the dark. By the time the clock struck 8:30, Grace Kingston was ready for action!

Alexandra, who had been watching from the sidelines while eating her lava cake, threw down the cake in frustration and stormed off.

"Fairies, thank you, thank you all for coming tonight!" said the announcer. "Another great season of Bankmant is right before our eyes! Katherine Globel is unfortunately sick. Instead, replacing her for tonight is Grace Kingston!"

The crowd of fairies cheered! As the applause died down, the announcer continued.

"First up are the Shimmering Hearts dancing in the water to 'Something Just Like This' by Coldplay and the Chainsmokers."

Four fairies entered the stadium and walked to the pool deck. They were each wearing a neon yellow swimsuit with a bright red heart on the front.

The announcer continued enthusiastically. "We have Clarissa Johnson."

One of the fairies did a quick wave to the crowd and then dived into the pool. "Next, Rose Churchill, Katie Wildflower, and

Alexandra Swamp."

Once the Shimmering Hearts completed their routine, it was time for Grace and the Golden Stars.

"Fairies, I present to you the Golden Stars!" The announcer said each of their names, and one by one they dove into the pool.

The audience cheered and clapped! All of a sudden, every light throughout the stadium went out. The clapping and cheering came to a halt. All Grace could see was a black figure flying above the dark stadium. Grace immediately jumped out of the pool with surprising ease. Something sparkly was all over Grace's bare legs.

"It must be the gel from the fairies' wings," thought Grace.

All of a sudden, Grace started floating in the air. She was flying! She realized that the chocolate lava cake that Alexandra had thrown down was on the pool deck. Grace snatched it. She had the best, craziest idea. Grace zoomed up to the dark figure in the air. She launched the cake out of her hands, right into its face. Revenge! Grace couldn't see his face, but Grace could tell from the hood that this mysterious figure was none other than Jacob Biforam.

Chapter Seven: The Performance

Grace snatched off Jacob's hood. She made him turn the stadium lights back on. Then, everyone saw him.

The next day, everything was cleared up. Apparently, the King of the Biforams had sent Jacob to sabotage the show to make the fairies mad. The Biforams were that mean! But Jacob was secretly a Bankmant fan. That is why he volunteered to do it. He wanted to watch how other fairies did it. But, he did have a punishment. His

punishment was to do the worst chore: taking out the garbage. He had to do that for one year.

In the evening, Grace was preparing the dessert. It was fudge. She was hoping that tonight there wouldn't be any more trouble! The fudge was a huge hit and so was Grace. Since they were unable to perform their routine the night before, the fairies had promised they would be able to perform tonight. As soon as Grace had eaten dinner, she went straight to the Bankmant stadium. The group practiced so hard! Finally, the time arrived! They dived into the pool without a problem. The music started. Grace and her team did a fabulous job and, because of that, they won first place! Grace had never been so happy in her life! She felt the joy, the happiness, and most importantly, the grace! At that exact moment, Grace realized why her parents named her Grace. Grace is another way of saying peaceful and happy. And for some reason, no matter where Grace was, she was always feeling that, and always will!

Pacing

Ailynn Knox-Collins taught Claire Wong to look closely at pacing and the use of white space while revising Claire's poem, "Silence."

Dear Reader,

Claire Wong's poem, "Silence," is a wonderful, emotion-provoking poem. Claire makes the reader think about what silence can mean to different people, or to each of us at different points in our lives. She makes the reader want to pay attention more to silence around us, and how it makes us feel.

When we worked on revision, Claire and I looked at pacing and the shape of the poem. *Pacing* encompasses a lot of elements, from the way a poem looks on the page, to the length of the lines, the word choices, and the punctuation. Pacing, used as a poet's tool, can control the way the poem is read. We examined how Claire's choice of words and the length of her phrases could guide the reader to pause at some points, and think about what's being communicated through the poem.

In learning about the use of white space, we looked at the impact that one word or phrase, placed on its own line, can make in a poem. We played around with putting the words all on one line, and then separating them. Then we looked at how this technique might help the reader speed up or slow down while reading. We discussed how the words had more or less power depending on where they are placed on the page. For example, in her original draft, Claire wrote:

Almost. Almost. Almost. Deafening.

This was one line. Then we separated them and made it read:

Almost. Almost.
Almost,
Deafening.

This slows the reader's eye and makes the reader feel the descent into the weight of silence, as it can sometimes feel. Also, the lines that contained only "Or" in them gave the reader time to transition from one experience of silence to the next, since each is totally different from the other. Finally, in the second stanza, the original version had this as its first line:

Silence, the golden sound of dawn and dusk.

Claire changed it to:

Silence.
The golden sound of
dawn
and
dusk.

First, this gave the poem a symmetry, since the first stanza also begins with one word: Silence. In this way, the poem is unified, and even though the second stanza is more about the general pictures of silence whereas the first is the more personal, there is a connection through these single words. The poem also ends with the word "Silence," bringing the entire picture to a close. Claire further chose to separate "dawn and dusk," thus leading the reader's eye down the page, as the sun would set at evening time.

When you are writing poetry, you might want to try Claire's approach to revision. Look at the words on your page and think about how you are guiding the readers' eyes across the poem, and how this might slow them down or speed them up. Think about how you want your readers to feel, and whether the shape of the poem helps them to get to that point. Even a slight change to a line can make all the difference.

Happy Writing,
Ailynn Knox-Collins

Ailynn Knox-Collins loves to read poetry and writes mostly about spaceships, strange new worlds, and aliens. Sometimes, she writes about pixie magic and ghosts, too. She has a series of books coming out in the Fall that are about living on Mars, in the far-off future, called Redworld. When she's not reading or writing, Ailynn is walking her three big dogs, or partnering with one of them, an Old English Sheepdog named Lady Rose, as a therapy team with Reading with Rover. She and Lady Rose love to listen to kids read to them at libraries and schools around Seattle.

Claire Wong

Claire is currently in fifth grade at Keys School and will be attending Castilleja School in the fall. She has a twin sister who was in Inklings 2014 and an adorable baby sister. Her favorite animal is an orca whale. Claire is also an avid reader. Her favorite school subjects are math, social studies, and art. Claire loves writing songs, poems, and fantasy stories in her free time.

Ailynn Knox-Collins: When did you start writing?

Claire Wong: Probably in the first grade. That's when I was getting interested in writing my own stories, and getting them published.

Q: What are you working on now?

A: This year, in English class, we're writing fractured fairy tales, and we'll be publishing that into a booklet. My story is a fractured version of "Sleeping Beauty" from Maleficent's point of view. The stories will be done by the end of the school year. At home, I'm writing a story called "The Lost Conductor of the Orchestra." The Orchestra plays to keep the harmony in balance in the world. The Conductor is the most important person and the current one is old and sick. He's going to die soon. So, they're holding a competition to find a new conductor, and it will be a kid. The main character, Violet, is an orphan. Her parents died in an earthquake. Violet knows that her dad used to work for the Orchestra, but she doesn't know what his job was. Her last memory was of the earthquake that killed him. I'm working on this book with my sister, Natalie. We've written about thirty-six pages already.

Q: How did you come up with the idea for your poem, "Silence"?
A: It's weird, but I was listening to the song "The Sound of Silence" from the movie *Trolls*, and I just started thinking about silence. I've written lots of poems for fun. They're about anything that comes to mind—from the pressure of taking tests to encouraging people to be themselves. The ideas just come to me while I'm listening to music or thinking about something. The ideas just come. Sometimes, I write stories, and when there are extra bits from the story that don't fit, I turn those bits into poems.

Q: How do you feel about your revision on the poem, "Silence"?
A: Revision has made it better. I know more about changing it to make it look cool. For me, revision makes my work stronger, which is good.

Silence

by
Claire Wong

Silence.

The absence of sound.

The sound of silence can be

So quiet, you can hear a pin drop.

Or

Everybody staring at you because you're the new kid.

Or

Fascination of a magical beast in front of you.

Or

Watching ripples echo across water.

Almost. Almost.

Almost,

Deafening.

Then you remember

It's

silence.

It echoes everywhere.

There, yet not there.

Existent, yet nonexistent.

Somewhere, yet nowhere.

Silence.

The golden sound of

Dawn

and

Dusk.

The mystifying sound of

Twilight

And

Midnight.

The sound of the moon rising.

The sound of the sun setting.

The sound of peace.

The sound of the end.

The sound of complete and total

Silence.

Character Detail

Madeline Knutson mentored Lauren Meier through a revision focused on fleshed-out characters in Lauren's story, "The Girl Who Was a Queen."

Dear Reader,

Lauren transcends the ordinary in her writing. She sets herself apart with her elaborately detailed style. As I read her story for the first time, I was transported gracefully from setting to setting due to her vivid imagery. After placing Lauren's manuscript down, I realized that Lauren writes with keen senses and incredible visualization skills.

However, I was eager to learn more about the characters that Lauren had started to develop. To take her story to the next level, I asked Lauren to apply the same level of description that appears in her settings to her characters. So, I wrote Lauren an editorial letter, firing off an extensive set of questions, asking her about specifics of each character (all whilst trying to avoid leading her choices). Then, for our Skype session, I took a more fun approach.

I believe that in order to generate new ideas, it is important to step away from the notepad, and participate in engaging, thought-provoking, and creative activities. I first asked Lauren to run around her house, finding objects that were meaningful to her. I explained that if Lauren ever felt stuck, she could simply look to her objects for inspiration. For example, she lifted her dog up to the webcam. Since Lauren has experience raising a dog, she can easily write about a character who is going through the same process. Furthermore, I was glad to get Lauren's blood pumping from quickly scavenging through her house, as exercise is known to have a positive effect on cognitive functioning.

Next, playing off of Lauren's strong imagination, we practiced guided visualization. In our guided visualization, we imagined a day in the life of one of her characters. Here is a sample of some of the questions I asked:

> *You're just waking up. What are you thinking? Can you remember your dreams? What is the first thing you see? What is the first thing you smell? You're getting ready for the day. What do you decide to wear? Take a moment to look in the mirror. Next, you head to the kitchen. Are you making breakfast? Does your character normally eat breakfast? Etc.*

After the visualization, I could see Lauren brimming with new creative ideas! Finally, I asked Lauren to draw and color her character.

Overall, I encouraged Lauren to visualize her characters from both an inner perspective (i.e. first person), as well as from an outer perspective (i.e. physical aspects, or how other characters relate to that chosen character). I asked her to imagine each character with immense detail, and wow! Lauren's story is now chock-full of detail!

As a mentor, I can only help Lauren develop the tools she needs to accomplish certain tasks, but it is up to Lauren to put in the work. Seeing Lauren's creative, funny, and moving finished product has made me eager to read more of her work, and I absolutely cannot wait to see one of her books on the *New York Times Best Sellers* list someday!

Sincerely,
Maddie Knutson

Madeline Knutson has been finding ways to create characters and tell stories since she can remember. She began by putting on plays for her neighborhood in her early years and turned to short story and poetry writing in her adolescence. Maddie returned to her love of theater and writing in college, earning her degree in theatre arts, and cultivating the art of grant writing at Santa Clara University. As a professional teaching artist and actress, Maddie believes that storytelling and creative writing are incredible tools for problem-solving, vocabulary expansion, communication, and of course imagination. Every child deserves a quality education through the arts, at least in her book.

Lauren Meier

Lauren is twelve, and has been reading and writing for years. She lives in Minnesota with her family and two dogs (who Elle's dogs are based on). When not reading or writing, she can be found shooting archery or doing her homework. If the whole writer thing doesn't work out, she wants to be a nurse.

Madeline Knutson: How did you come up with the character of Elle?
Lauren Meier: I came up with this idea of a girl who dreams of becoming a princess and later becomes the queen of her own kingdom. The rest just kind of came naturally when I was writing.

Q: When did you first start writing?
A: I think I started writing in first grade.

Q: Who do you enjoy sharing your stories with?
A: I don't really share my stories with a lot of people, but when I do, I share them with my family.

Q: What's your writing process like? Do you have any rituals?
A: I get an idea, and sometimes I'll write a mini-backstory for the characters. I'll usually have a basic idea of what I want the storyline to be, but not always. After I write the first few paragraphs introducing

the reader to the characters and setting, the rest just kind of flows organically.

Q: What advice would you give to other young writers?
A: First, editing may be really hard, and it may seem pointless and frustrating, but it's worth it, because it really does improve your story. Second, this is going to sound cliché, but practice does make perfect! I was really, really bad when I first began writing, and now I'm not really, really bad. I've been writing a lot–and I mean a lot–since I began, and my writing has improved so much.

The Girl Who Was a Queen

by
Lauren Meier

Hi, my name is Eleanor (Elle for short). But you can call me Your Royal Highness. I'm a queen. I know I'm a queen. It's just all the world ever sees is a stupid little girl with stupid little fantasies.

But I like to sit up high on a hill on warm summer nights. On these nights, I escape to whole new world: a world of fairies and elves and witches and mermaids, a world where I'm queen. A world where the king of the giants bows down to me, and my palace is made of sparkling pixie dust.

But in reality, people just say "Mmhmm, that's nice. What are your *actual* goals?" when they ask what I want to be when I grow up and I say "a queen."

In my kingdom, my sister Olive's obnoxious boyfriend is banished and my sister begs me to let him return but I say, "No."

Olive is short and skinny with long, dark brown hair. She's a girly girl, and spends a whole hour every morning doing her hair. Her boyfriend has shaggy auburn hair, and an obsession with *Star Wars*. I

don't like him because he always nags me to spell better even though he has awful grammar, even worse than mine. Have you heard him speak? Awful grammar, especially since he's eighteen years old and I'm ten.

But my sister, Lizzy, has a boyfriend named Webster and he can stay. Lizzy isn't the best at math, and she has a tutor. Long story short, Olive thought that Webster was Lizzy's tutor when they first met.

She was very confused when my mom told her that they were dating, and she loudly exclaimed, "Why is Lizzy dating her tutor?"

It made things kind of awkward, and Webster had to explain that even though he was good at math, and Lizzy isn't, he is not her tutor. Lizzy is constantly dyeing her hair a new color, and has a nose ring. He doesn't nag me for my spelling even though his is impeccable. Webster is what most people would call a nerd, glasses and all. He wants to be a cardiologist someday.

I like to pretend to be swimming with mermaids in the beautiful blue waters of the Frozen Sea, escaping under the surface and floating in a frozen paradise, the water chilling me all over, but really I'm just taking a cold bath.

My sister Victoria is the only person who believes me. She likes to read books about magic and kings and countesses and elves and wizards, books like *The Chronicles of Narnia* and *Alice in Wonderland* and *The Wizard of Oz*.

"Don't worry, Elle. I believe you," she told me once.

We were up in a tree, and I was telling her about how no one believed me when I said I was a queen. She had helped me scale the tree. A pile of books rested on a forked branch. They were bent and dog-eared from years of being read again and again.

"Really?" I asked, unsure.

"Really," she replied.

A bird chirped loudly a foot above us, and I screamed, startled. Victoria laughed, and handed me *Grimms' Fairy Tales.* I flipped to "The Sleeping Beauty," page 42, and all my problems disappeared.

My pet pug, Prince, is the heir to my throne. He's white, with brown spots, and he loves tennis balls, and he smells like, well, dog. Once I retire, I have to leave my kingdom to someone I trust, and my pug is the only one who makes the cut and believes in me (besides my mastiff, Dame Heidi, but she's too busy fighting off evil sorcerers).

Dame Heidi, my big, black, furry dog, is my protector. She fights off evil witches for me. Everyone else just calls her Heidi (except for Victoria), but I'm Heidi's favorite. I like to curl up on her and she puts her massive head on my belly.

Days and weeks and months and years have passed. Even though three sisters, my mom, my dad, ten teachers, and a school counselor say I should have forgotten being queen by now, I haven't.

In fact, I've only become *more* sure of my royal status. I truly am a queen—not just a little girl with a title and palace, but a ruler.

I can practically hear the crowds chanting, "All hail Queen Elle! All hail Queen Elle!"

I mean, c'mon, I finally have followers! (The fact that I told them that I was going to buy them a new car if they became my loyal subject is not important.) Not just Victoria and my dogs. No, I have a sea of mermaids, armies of knights and warriors, and hundreds of

thousands of peasants. The only thing we need is a place to live: a territory, a country. We can't keep living in the suburbs. People think I'm "weird" and "delusional" and "should seek professional help." There are hundreds of tiny, unpopulated islands in the world to conquer (and island-dwelling would be fantastic for the mermaid population), but I want my people to be united, and no tiny island can hold us all. Besides, there's a reason they're unpopulated!

We can't live on Antarctica, because they have laws against permanent and political dwellings and military usage, whatever. All I know is we can get in trouble with the UN.

We can build a floating island and roam the seas as one nation, but I think that's illegal. Or we could buy some property in the desert or something and build a city, but the mermaids wouldn't like that. They prefer the ocean with its rainbow coral and honestly, I don't blame them. Besides, they can't breathe above water for very long. The mermaids are beautiful, with long, jet black hair, porcelain skin, and pretty blue eyes. They're experts on sailing and fish, which should be very beneficial for food production and shipping. Surprisingly, they know a lot about accounting and bookkeeping, so I'll never have to do any math myself. The Royal Bookkeeping Office is going to be half-underwater, half-above water, so they can work comfortably, and we humans can breathe.

Wait! Hold up! I've got it! We should buy some land in, like, Florida or Oregon or somewhere with a coast and build a big city there! I can see it now: a huge park in the center, a lavish Royal Palace, skyscrapers, a thriving Main Street, a garden with grapes that taste like pure delight.

I can practically hear the joyful clitter-clatter of the peasants' feet on the sidewalks! Now all I need to do is find some land for sale on the coast, buy it, get some papers, and plan it out! I have to go on vacation, err, check the climate first, though. Whatever you call it, it's coming out of the taxpayers' dollars, along with my five-star hotel room.

I snuggle with a sleeping Dame Heidi and my pug, who keeps trying to lick my face, and who seems to be biased toward the warmer states, as I scout out real estate online, then write tedious emails to the US Pentagon, then make the transaction, then fill out paperwork for the UN, then post on Twitter about it, and then start planning my city. Finally!

I once again sit on top of the hill, dreaming of a land where there's endless clear blue water to swim in and there's the most delicious grapes on earth and I rule. But this time it's different. This time it's going to come true! The architects that I hired are working on my palace at this very minute. I mean, my city smells like cement right now, but it's temporary. The architects are—thankfully—temporary, too.

"You're absolutely crazy," they told me when I described my vision for the kingdom.

"Really? Would a crazy person have several hundred thousand loyal subjects?" I responded, annoyed.

"I heard you bought them all cars as a bribe."

"How I recruited them isn't important," I said, changing the subject back to my plans.

I can practically see the children running past my palace, the warm breeze floating through my window as I perch on my throne, and the mermaids swimming around in the fountains. I can almost hear the peasants at work, and the teachers teaching, and the students not

paying attention but goofing off. Alas, it's not real—not yet.

Finally, the day arrives, and my kingdom is ready. My subjects move in by the hundred, and they, too, are amazed by our lovely city. The mermaids are shocked. We built them their very own beach, and the peasants enjoy the lovely central park. Of course, we have state-of-the-art military facilities, so if we ever do have to fight, we're ready. I have a bulletproof stained glass wall built around the city, but we need great technology, too. I mean, if we ever do go to war with the US, we need to be prepared to defeat one of the best militaries in the world, and a protective/decorative wall is not going to defeat them— which is why I built a big fortress for the military.

Did I mention my palace is made of marble? Or that I have my very own silver throne? I even have a balcony with a mini-throne on it, so even the clouds bow down to me! My bedroom has only the best cherry wood furniture, too. All of the chandeliers have teardrop-shaped diamonds, and little silver hearts, not to mention they smell heavenly.

But my favorite part of the whole kingdom is the park. It has warthogs, birds imported from the Caribbean, all sorts of gazelles and antelope, bamboos that came all the way from the local zoo, the chameleon from Madagascar, and tortoises.

Of course, I have a new heir to the crown: The General Cornelius White. Our wedding is scheduled for next fall. Cornelius is not only hilarious, but he's somehow managed to command an army of 25,000 all by himself. In addition, he saved the life of one of the tortoises in the park, who was stepped on by a horse. How can you not fall for him?

Of course, it is going to be grand. The whole kingdom is invited, and they're going to be shocked when they see I had diamond vases made for centerpieces, and I'm putting pretty pink roses in them. The cake is going to be thirteen layers, light pink and white, with pink frosting roses that taste like strawberries. Oh, and the dress! It's a lace ball gown, with a twenty-foot train. It has pearl buttons, and it'll be sprayed with lavender perfume, made from real lavender. We're having punch, and steak, and lemonade. I'm salivating already! I'm having the cook perfect her steak, which, to be honest, tastes like charcoal right now. In all honesty, a lot of her food tastes like charcoal. One of the reasons I haven't fired her is that her cake is *amazing*, and she's also my grandma, and I can't fire my grandma.

To think this all started with a girl with a dream.

Character Development

Ernesto Cisneros mentored Zachary Marinov through a revision focused on showing the unique perspective of a character in Zachary's story, "The Skeleton."

Dear Reader,

Writing a suspenseful story can be a challenging task—even for professional writers. There are so many elements that need to be done well for the story to work. Zachary's story, "The Skeleton," is original in that it portrays the tragic side of a character whose perspective we don't normally get to see—the Grim Reaper himself, Death.

The early line, *"it takes some self-persuasion and much remorse to carry out the job . . ."* shows Death's very human side. It is here that we begin to see the character presented in a new, almost positive light. Zachary actually manages to make the reader feel bad for Death—this is no easy task.

Part of the revision process was helping Zachary to streamline his story by taking out some of the extra details that took us away from the heart of the story. Once this was done, he went back and provided more backstory to help the reader understand the motivation for Death's actions, thus allowing them to better connect with him.

Zachary worked very hard on making the short story a bit clearer while still managing to maintain the story's dark mysterious feel. I not only enjoyed re-reading each draft, but listening to his excitement about the tale. I would offer one piece or advice to any aspiring author—be enthused about what you write. You will be spending *a lot* of time alone with your story, so make sure you write about characters and storylines that are meaningful and entertaining to you.

Remember, the best stories are not written—they are revised.

Happy writing,
Ernesto Cisneros

Ernesto Cisneros was born in the gang-ridden and often marginalized part of Santa Ana. By adolescence, he began questioning his place in the world. In his senior year in high school, he discovered a love of literature that continued to grow. However, it was not until he began teaching kids with similar backgrounds to himself that he learned about the value and need for literary diversity. And that is when he began writing books for children. He believes in creating realistic (often flawed) characters with everyday struggles. His book, *The Writing on the Wall*, is the fictional but very personal story of his life growing up on Santa Ana. Learn more about Ernesto's work at *www.ernestocisneros.com*.

Zachary Marinov

Zachary is a seventh grader at Avery Coonley. When not traveling, he enjoys reading, building robots, and playing volleyball. His favorite vacation spot has been visiting London, England because of its amazing history and places to visit. Furthermore, he has a passion for math, and has competed in many math competitions and Olympiads. In addition, he enjoys learning new languages such as Mandarin, French, and Latin.

Ernesto Cisneros: Is there a section of your story that you are most proud of? If so, why?

Zachary Marinov: I do not think that there is just one section that I am most proud of, but I think the entire story overall is much better than before the revisions.

Q: What was the most difficult part of writing your story?

A: The most difficult part of writing the story was writing the ending, because I did not know how to end the story in a satisfying way that fit with how I had written it.

Q: What was the most difficult part of revising your story?

A: The most difficult part of revising the story was determining the exact backstory of the main character that would make sense and allow the reader to best understand Death's actions.

Q: Your final draft is much different from your original story. How do you feel the revisions helped your story?

A: I think the revisions helped my story by providing more of a backstory for the reader, to understand the cause of Death's actions, and allowing them to understand him more, and connect with him.

Q: How did you work on strengthening your character through your revisions?

A: I worked on strengthening my character through the revisions by providing more of a backstory for the character, so that the reader could understand why the main character acted as he did.

The Skeleton

by

Zachary Marinov

Every time I wonder about why I am pictured so odiously, a black cape-cloaked skeleton with a scythe, I think back to all the reasons why I exist. The reasons why that skeleton travels along the River Styx, retrieving pleading souls from the "whips and scorns of time," as my friend Hamlet once said.

He, out of many, embraced me when his time came, as the thread of life thinned in him, until it vanished. Most times, people will me to take them away, but when they don't, when they steadfastly, stoically grip to life, it takes some self-persuasion and much remorse to carry out the job . . .

Wake up. Last-minute preparations. Breakfast. School. Bus. London! The day's events raced by, aiming to outrun each other. The boy's excitement threatened to race along with them, leaving him standing by the curb under droplets of rain, his mien the mirror image of his surroundings. That is how he would have liked his day to go: anything better than the awry occurrence that seemed all too

stochastic. How he probably remembers it is in a few screams of panic, as he struggled to make sense of the gouts of water that fell like juggernauts from the now hostile sky. A high-pitch nasal voice howled out the evening news:

A freak monsoon hit London. At 18:17, a small cloud hovered in the sky. It gradually released a fine drizzle of rain: everybody and everything continued to carry out their business. Suddenly, a mere five minutes later, it had been entirely forgotten about, considered to be the meaningless first wave of an attack.

Once it had passed, a colossal cloud enveloped the first, successfully blotting out the beauty of the sunset in one loathsome motion. The darkness it brought transferred itself into intermittent, sporadic waves of panic when a mighty, freak monsoon had caught London by surprise. At that time, a family had been on the London Eye, enjoying a full view of all London had to offer; nothing could have been better until . . . the sky blacked out. Screams from below resounded. Great raindrops, the size of buckets, fell out of the gloom. Wind buffeted the pod they were in, as . . .

The radio announcer spoke further, but I drowned out the noise. I knew what had happened. That boy now lay in agony upon the sidewalk, crushed beneath a fallen streetlight. I came gently, but he seemed to sense my presence. Bawling, he resisted. Every time I came closer, he shrieked and begged to live longer without even knowing for certain that I was coming for him. Let me reassure you, I didn't want to do it; I didn't want to take another soul. I don't have a proclivity to take lives. Yet I didn't want to see this kind-faced boy in anguish any longer. I'd deliberated too much. In one swift motion, I swept up his soul. Stood up. Looked. Wept.

Instantaneously, a motley assortment of people who I later found out to be his family appeared out of the gloom. They swarmed around me like bees environing an oppressor who had wronged them. Their weeping told me it must have been for the boy. Their size amplified to much greater proportions as a crowd of other Londoners amalgamated to their cause.

My heart—if I have one, as I don't know—pounded with a tremendous force as it turned to lead. I don't remember much from this moment, other than me being in a state of shock. Shoes clapped on the road. The remorse was deafening. I stumbled.

"Stop, stand back!"

I had been deeply affected by that occurrence, and still am.

Racing away while I tried to remain calm, I noticed the snow from the night before. It lay innocently before the destruction around, and was anything but diaphanous. It had been ground to a fine pulp by the plethora of boots which had crushed it so many times that it had capitulated immediately, and was darkening at the edges, the mud from the gutters working its way gradually, arduously, to the core of every piece. I felt like the snow then, as I do now: remorse and regret working its way into me, while I begin to understand why I am a black-caped skeleton.

Amplifying Your Premise

Dear Reader,

In "Seeing Colors," Lauren Crawford crafted a gorgeous fantasy with a powerful and sophisticated voice. Her premise is intriguing: that a life without hope is gray, whereas a life with hope is filled with color.

For Lauren's revision, we focused on amplifying your premise. When I read her story, I loved her *big idea* (or premise) that color equals hope, that you need to live a hopeful life even in times of despair, and that once you give up hope, you give up on living. I suggested that Lauren amplify this idea by reinforcing moments where Anika isn't hopeful and the world is gray versus the times when Anika is hopeful and she glimpses bits of color.

For example, in Lauren's original draft, her first chapter (after the prologue) started with:

I lay down by the Old Oak Tree, expecting Mama to be home

soon. The sharp rocks jab into my skin. Seconds pass, then minutes, then hours. Every time I hear the town bell ring, I start to lose hope. It has been a few days since Mama has disappeared. My eyes swell with tears. I know I can't keep the tears back. So I close my eyes.

We talked about how there was perhaps too much hope in this paragraph for her "gray" world. Here is how Lauren changed that opening:

> *I lie down by the Old Oak Tree. Its trunk is as gray as dust. The sharp rocks jab into my skin. Seconds pass, then minutes, then hours. It's been a few days since Mama has disappeared. My eyes swell with tears. I know I can't keep the tears back. So I close my eyes.*

Notice that she added a "gray" description about the Old Oak Tree. She also removed her main character's hopeful thoughts. By amplifying her premise, Lauren amplifies her main character's hopelessness, which brings that character into sharper focus for the readers. In another great example (in the fourth chapter), Lauren originally wrote:

> *I look into the tiny man's eyes. They twinkle a familiar twinkle. Where have I seen it? It fills me with hope. I think, I think hard. I think of signs of love in my life. Then I have it.*

We talked about adding a smidge of color to amplify Lauren's premise that color and hope go together. Here is the rewrite:

> *I look into the tiny man's eyes. They twinkle a familiar twinkle. Specks of gold grace the outside of his eyes. Where have I seen it? It fills me with hope. I think, I think hard. I think of signs of love in my life. Then I have it.*

By adding in those specks of gold, Lauren managed to reinforce her story premise and in the process, make her story stronger.

To amplify your premise, first you need to figure out what your premise is! If you aren't sure what your premise is, consider brainstorming with your parents, a teacher, or a friend. Another way to identify your premise is to think about what promise you are trying to make to your reader. The most satisfying stories make a promise to the reader upfront, and then deliver on that promise by the end. In "Seeing Colors," the promise is that the main character is going to see the world mostly in gray until she has grown more hopeful and resilient. Only then will she be able to see the world in full color.

I hope this concept of amplifying your premise resonates with you. Having a strong premise hooks your reader. Amplifying that premise throughout your story keeps them reading till the very end!

Happy writing,
Kristi Wright

Kristi Wright is the Assistant Regional Advisor for the San Francisco/South region of the Society of Children's Books Writers and Illustrators. She offers writing workshops at the elementary school level with a focus on point of view and sensory detail. She is also the assistant editor for a blog that analyzes middle grade novels as mentor texts for writers: *www.mglunchbreak.com*. Her indie-published futuristic middle grade adventure series, *The Basker Twins in the 31st Century*, raises funds and awareness for a rare, childhood-onset disease, Friedreich's ataxia. Find her at *www.kristiwrightauthor.com* and on Twitter @KristiWrite.

Lauren Crawford

Lauren is ten years old and heading into fifth grade at Sacred Heart School. She lives in Atherton, California with her parents, Renee and David; her older brother, James; and her Goldendoodle, Cody. In her free time, she loves to sing and write songs. She also enjoys playing tennis and drawing. If she could visit anywhere, she'd visit Rome, Italy, because of its energy and history. Her favorite colors are black and white, and her favorite food is ice cream.

Kristi Wright: What inspired you to write "Seeing Colors"?
Lauren Crawford: I really like writing about deep meanings. One time I wondered, "What is the meaning of life?" My mom told me that no one really knows, but she suggested that we were put on Earth to make it a better place. I thought: What if there's a girl who hasn't found the true meaning of life yet, and she goes on this journey to try to find it, and it's not what she expects?

Q: What was the hardest part of writing a fantasy?
A: I feel like when you are writing a biography, you know how everything was because you were there. But when you are writing a fantasy, you have to put yourself in your character's position and think about her world, and how she would react and think.

Q: Did your story change when you amplified your premise?
A: Yes, definitely. I had written this story a little while ago. When I read it over, it was a totally different story in my mind. I tried to put all my thoughts in the story, and when I put them in, it made more sense because no one knew those thoughts except for me.

Q: Do you like how the story changed?
A: I do. I feel like I got to share a lot more about what I was thinking with the reader, which made the story less confusing.

Q: Did anything surprise you during the revision process?
A: Well, it kind of surprised me. Before I started the revision process, I was really satisfied with my story. But when my mentor pointed things out, I realized that the story could be much better. I could fix that, and fix that, etc.

Q: What did you learn from this revision process that you can use as you write your next story?
A: I learned to tell the reader enough information so they aren't confused, but not to tell them all of it so they still have to read till the end of the story. I tried to put the reader in the character's position and make them connect with the character.

Q: What's your favorite part of "Seeing Colors"?
A: From a writing perspective, I liked when the main character was in the middle of her adventures. I liked putting obstacles in front of her. But as a reader, I really liked reading my introduction—the prologue. I was really proud of it.

Q: What advice would you give other writers about revision?
A: I didn't initially want to revise my story. I thought it would be a lot of work. But if you truly love writing, it's actually really fun. I'm really happy with how my story turned out.

Q: Are you writing anything right now?
A: I've been really busy since it's the end of the year. I think the summer would be a great time to write another story. I'm writing a song right now that kind of tells a story. Not about a girl, but more life lesson-y.

Seeing Colors

by

Lauren Crawford

Introduction

The things I am about to tell you are not about someone who lives a perfect life. It is not about someone who has somebody to watch over her. It is about real life. Something that is bittersweet. Something that is not forgiving. Life has some very happy people in it. But of course, there are also some people who struggle. There is nothing I can say to prepare you for this book. So if you are not someone who likes to face reality, please do not read on. I am about to tell you about a girl who is now a woman. But only because of the things she has gone through, not because of her perfections. The past has changed her in many ways. She has been scarred, and her scars are what make her human.

All she sees in the world is gray. Do not be mistaken; she is not colorblind. Color is hope.

Chapter One

I lie down by the Old Oak Tree. Its trunk is as gray as dust. The sharp rocks jab into my skin. Seconds pass, then minutes, then hours. It's been a few days since Mama has disappeared. My eyes swell with tears. I know I can't keep the tears back. So I close my eyes.

My eyelids flutter as my weary eyes notice something: a necklace, Mama's necklace, lying there on the cold hard ground. I put it around my neck. I remember the times I put my face in Mama's chest when I was sad. It would always be there, hanging around her neck. The words stick in my mind. "You can never try too hard," it said. I run my fingers over the words, engraved in pure gold.

"Anika, sometimes when you try, things get worse. But trust me, eventually, it's the right path to go," Mama would say.

It's impossible for me to believe her. Papa is gone, and he isn't coming back. I remember the moment I found out. Ice cold words coming out of my mother's lips. "Cancer." All I wanted to do was cling to Mama. I didn't want to lose her, too. I didn't want to get out of bed, I didn't want to help with dinner, and I didn't want to go outside and play like I used to.

I hear the town bells: ring, ring, ring. I start to realize the truth. Mama is gone. Like Papa. I feel helpless. I ask the Old Oak Tree, "Where is she?" Usually, he answers me in my heart with a small tingle telling me that everything is fine. But this time, I feel nothing.

Chapter Two

I bend down on my knees and cry. With each sob, my shoulders rock back and forth. I can't believe it. I won't. Mama and I have been through too much together to just let go. I know she would want me to go find her. No matter what anyone says, I won't give up. I will try, just like Mama's necklace told me to. Every journey has to start somewhere, and I guess this is where mine does.

Finally, I stand up, kissing the Old Oak Tree's scars. I look at him one more time with hopeful eyes, but he continues to stand there, tall and proud, just like Papa. No matter who stood in his way, he would stay strong. I wish I could be like that. I'm nothing. A gray ghost in a gray world.

I take my last look at my town. It looks like the usual. Fruit and vegetable stands lining the dirt pathway. Houses behind them in a perfect line. Yet our town is far from perfect. Everyone is sad. Papa would tell me stories about how the town used to be. When he and Mama met, everyone was cheerful and happy. But then people started getting laid off. People started losing their homes and had to live on the street. My family was one of them. Now, not everyone has the basic things a person needs to be happy. So they aren't, and that brings the once-beautiful town down.

I make a final decision to go find Mama. I turn to the ragged hills. Mama's favorite spot. I remember we would have picnics with Papa. We would laugh so hard that we forgot about our struggles. I loved laughing. I loved the feeling it gave me. I remember the taste of Mama's turkey sandwiches. I miss them. Ever since Papa died, she isn't the same. And neither are the woods. There are no more picnics, no more laughing, and the woods now frighten me. Without all the happy times we had there, they seem lifeless.

I have a feeling that something is going to go wrong. But I can't disappoint Mama. So I will search for her in the woods. If I don't

find her, maybe it will bring me closer to her in the long run. I take a deep breath, but then I feel something, a strange feeling that I can't quite put to words. But it feels rather nice. I hear something drop. It is an apple. But as soon as I pick it up, it turns red!

I remember this color. The village would be lined with fruits and vegetable stands. Apples, bell peppers, tomatoes, and strawberries. They were all red. Red can be sirens, blood, or a sign to stop. But red is also the color of your heart, and Mama's favorite color. Red is also a warm fire, protecting you from all bad things. Oh, I remember red, and the day it disappeared.

I glance back at the apple. It looks so sweet and vibrant that I just have to take a bite. When I take a bite, it tastes the same. Yet the color does something to the apple that I simply can't explain. It fills me with pleasure and happiness. But then I feel another feeling. A feeling that I am familiar with. Pain. It is my head.

Chapter Three

"Hey, where you going, Anika?"

Randy, I say to myself. I don't reply. It hurts me to say that I am afraid but I am.

"I said, 'Where are you going?'" he yells.

"To find my mom," I say quietly.

"Ha," Randy snickers. "You'll never find your mom or be someone or something. You're just a little brat."

I look down at the floor and see the color red again, on a rather small stone. But this red fills me with a different emotion. It looks like cruelty. Am I nothing but a little brat? Will I always be this way? Will the dreams I dream never become a reality? I look down at my mother's necklace and hear her voice cheering me on. I need to hear her voice again. No.

I pull my head up and smile at him and say, "Thank you."

He looks confused, but now I am not.

Chapter Four

The forest ground will be hard on my feet and I know it. But even though I am discouraged, I must go on.

I start to enter the main part of the forest where Mama, Papa, and I would have our picnics. But I notice something. There is a gate. I know, right? How did a gate get in the middle of the forest? But I decide to take it in as something that I could easily find here. Maybe that will change my luck. I touch the brim of the gate to make sure it is actually there. I confirm with myself that I am not hallucinating. But then I hear a small but certainly not quiet voice.

"Hey, what are you doing here?"

I jerk my head up in surprise. Standing there is a tiny, little man but he sends chills down my spine. He reminds me of a story Papa told me called *The Wizard of Oz*. He is like the man at Emerald City who wouldn't let Dorothy and her friends pass.

This man at the gate frightens me. He has a turned-up nose and a big belly. He wears a big top hat that covers his hair. That is, if he has any. I have never seen someone so small, but somehow he looks familiar.

The tiny man sees the fear in my eyes and his voice seems to soften a little bit. "It's okay, I'm not going to hurt you." His voice helps

but I am still frightened. "You want to pass, eh? Well, hate to break it to ya, kid, but it's not that simple," he says. "I'll try to make it as easy as I can for ya. Just answer my question and you can go through."

"Okay," I say. That doesn't sound so hard. I mean, all I have to do is answer one question.

"What is love to you?" he asks.

I don't really know what to say. I have never thought about this much. You can't do this, I say to myself. You're unlovable. Why else do you think Mama left?

I look him in the eyes. "Could you please just let me pass?"

"Sorry, kid. Rules are rules, and I've made it as simple as I can for ya."

I stare down at the dirt. Guess this is where it all ends. I'm so stupid. I can't believe I thought I could find her. I look into the tiny man's eyes. They twinkle a familiar twinkle. Specks of gold grace the outside of his eyes. Where have I seen it? It fills me with hope. I think, I think hard. I think of signs of love in my life. Then I have it.

"Love is what I feel for the Old Oak Tree. Love is the fact that I can tell him all of my secrets and I know that I can trust him," I say. "Love is why I am struggling to find my mom, and love is why I am not quitting. Love is what I feel for my father and the times he felt the same. Love is . . ." but then I stop, for I am interrupted, not by the tiny man, but by myself.

I am interrupted by something I had felt but had disappeared that same second. Yet the feeling stuck within my bones, and I knew now. I was always loved. Love doesn't go away even though Papa died.

I look up at the man. He is all smiles. I take a moment to admire his beautiful teeth just like Mama's. He pulls a lever and the doors of the gate swing open. I am shocked, but at the same time proud. It makes me feel confident.

In that moment, the man and the gate vanish. The forest disappears, and there a town appears. Now, I know what you're thinking: what's so special about a town? At first, I think the same thing. But it fills me with the same feeling that the tiny man had given me, only stronger. Then, before my eyes, I see something. Pink.

Chapter Five

Children are skipping and singing and sharing, not just food but kindness. One child gives another child half of her bread. Another person makes a child a picture. All the younger children are holding hands and singing "Ring Around the Rosie." I think back to my village. Why couldn't my village be like that?

All of a sudden, the singing, dancing, and sharing stops. Everyone grows silent. I don't understand. Why have they stopped?

Suddenly the silence is broken with screams of terror. All the children and their mothers run off into different directions. Where should I go? Should I be afraid of whatever they are running from? I look around helplessly but see nobody to turn to. Suddenly adrenaline kicks into my veins. I run as fast as I can all the way back to the gate, but it is gone, and so is all my hope. I feel a dark feeling inside. Like my mom is growing farther away from me every time I try. When I try harder, things only grow worse. I just want to quit. But that's what I've been doing my whole life when something is too hard. I can't this time.

I look around frantically to find some place to rest my feet. I look up at the sky and see colors, colors I am familiar with. Red, pink, but one I haven't seen in a long time: orange. It makes me feel my mom's hugs that give that warmth when I need it, and I need it bad. It fills me with a light that can block out any darkness.

Chapter Six

On and on I walk, only growing colder. Every step I take, it seems like the forest is getting more and more lifeless. But then I hear something, a crash of some sort. Heavy drops of rain fall on my body stinging with cold, thunder. I can't go on farther. But I still won't give up. My mom is out there, and I won't let her die. That is, unless I die. But I won't. I start to think back and regret my coming here. Maybe mom is back at home with the Old Oak Tree. Maybe she is worried about me. I am completely lost.

Exhausted, I lie on the hard ground and drift into a dream. In my dream, I look around and see life, like a butterfly taking its first flight. Then a voice whispers to me.

"Live," it says. I don't understand who "it" is or what "it" means. But in that very second, the dream is over and I wake up. But the once-dead forest is green. Just like the one in my dream. Life is everywhere. We never have this at home. I stroke the branches of an old pine. There are still raindrops that grace its bark. But then something happens. Snap!

Chapter Seven

I tumble to the ground, aching in pain. My head is throbbing in dismay and all I want to do is lie here and cry. My hip is sore and I can't feel my legs. I gather all my strength to lift my head up and see what hit me—a tree branch. Luckily, it isn't big enough to pin me to the ground forever, but it still hurts, a lot. I push as hard as I can, like a gigantic sit-up. I was never good at these. Finally, I thrust the branch off me. I am relieved but at the same time completely shocked. I take a moment and close my eyes. I picture myself running into my mom's warm arms. She embraces me softly and fills me with love.

I snap myself out of it. If my mom is really out there, she wouldn't want me to daydream about finding her; she would want me to actually find her. I try to ignore the pain. Every step I take, I picture her waiting for me at the top of the mountain. I limp all the way to a meadow where I tumble to the ground in relief. Suddenly I feel light and the pain is gone.

Then, specks of yellow appear in the grass. Yellow. But out of the corner of my eye, I see a bunny. Two bunnies. A baby and its mother. A familiar feeling fills my body. A feeling I have the exact words for. Sadness. Tears fill my eyes until the voices come back, the voices of the bullies. I blink, and everything seems darker.

You'll never be someone or something. You're just a little brat. Give up. Please just go away. Not here, not now.

I look at my hands and they're filled with tears. I see my reflection in the crystal blue water. Blue. I know this feeling, but the color I am not aware of. It fills me with a sadness that cannot be tamed. But I won't give up, not now. I have come too far. I have conquered too much to stop. Even if I never find my mom, I will be strong, I am strong. And I will stay strong. Just the thought of food makes hunger fill me within a second. I crave it. I need it. Right as I think it, I see it.

Purple, a color that is so beautiful. It is a plum. As I am just

about to grab one of those plums, my mom's necklace starts to glow until a figure appears. My mom appears. I run up to her and hug her tight.

I ask, "Where have you been? Did someone take you or perhaps you got lost or…"

She stops me there. She says, "You have found life, my darling."

"What do you mean, Mama? I have always known what life is."

"I was the bully and I was the man working the gate," Mama says. "I was the dream and the bunny and its mother," she says. "Because of that, you have found all of the colors. Papa may be gone. Trust me, I am just as sad as you are. That is no reason to stop living. Take a look at the world that was once gray, and now take a real look at the world. Do you understand me, my darling?"

"Yes," I reply. "This is the meaning of life."

Then I look up at the sky and see a rainbow—not a gray one, a real one. I love rainbows. Each color is beautiful in its own way. But rainbows are when all those beautiful colors come together. Suddenly the color from the rainbow drains out into the world and disappears.

It is just as if Papa was standing right next to me. My world is now filled with different shades and I know. I understand why. I didn't go on this trip to find my mom. I did this to find the true meaning of life.

"Oh, dear child, come home now, to your real home and live the way you are meant to live."

So I did. And ever since that day, I have been seeing colors.

Figurative Language

Dear Reader,

In Toby Jacob's poem, "Storm," she used the metaphor of a storm to create an effect of emotions swirling and the reader tumbling from line to line. She starts with two questions, and then a few short lines. From my first read of the poem, the effect of these initial lines was a feeling of the poem ramping up in energy and intensity, similar to the way wind builds at the beginning of a storm.

As we worked through our revision, we looked at figurative language. Most of Toby's images related to a storm, but a few did not. As we considered how to amplify the effect of the storm building, pausing in the middle of the poem as the eye of the storm swept over, and then blowing past in the end, we decided to remove most of the unrelated images.

Notice that word: "most." Toby carefully considered every line in her poem and chose which lines to keep and which to remove or replace. She did what poets do, which is to weigh each word against the feeling she hoped to create in her reader. In the end, Toby chose what to keep and what to change based on her intended outcome.

If you're working on a poem with a central image, and like Toby, hope to create a powerful emotional experience for your reader, try these steps:

1. Decide what effect you would like to create.
2. Think about how the images in your poem can amplify the effect you hope to create.
3. Consider the pacing of each line. How can you use length of lines and line breaks to speed up or slow down your poem?
4. Look for lines or images that aren't needed. Sometimes the best way to amplify a feeling in a poem is to remove the pieces that aren't helping to create that effect.
5. Read your poem out loud, and ideally, to a friend. Discuss the way the poem sounds and feels. Make final adjustments based on what you notice.

It was a joy to work with Toby. I was very impressed with her dedication, creativity, and the courage with which she put her feelings on the page. Prepare to be swept away by Toby's "Storm"!

My best,
Naomi Kinsman

Naomi Kinsman is the author of the *From Sadie's Sketchbook* series and the award-winning *Spilled Ink, a Writer's Commonplace Book*. Most recently, Naomi co-authored the *Glimmer Girls* series with recording artist, Natalie Grant. Through a decade of writing and directing plays for young people, and serving as a resident artist in classrooms across the country, Naomi developed Writerly Play, which uses game-based strategies and tools to teach young writers. Naomi also founded Society of Young Inklings. She holds a BA in Theatre Arts from Seattle Pacific University and an MA in Writing for Children and Young Adults from Hamline University.

Toby Jacob

Toby lives in a nice yellow house in a small city that can't be found on a map. She enjoys reading, writing, and hanging out with her friends. Her favorite classes in school include social studies and writing. She hopes that you enjoyed her poem.

Naomi Kinsman: You've written a poem about strong feelings. How do you choose topics to write about?

Toby Jacob: You have to choose something that's important to you and that has affected you positively or negatively. When that light bulb in your head starts blinking, just go for it. It's good to get your feelings on paper.

Q: We added more storm images into your poem in the revision process. How did you go about making changes?

A: You have to unify your piece with a focus so the reader can really feel what's going on. You want to help your reader see what you're seeing, and to feel what you're feeling, and to give them a fishbowl-look into your experience.

There is a flow that every poem has, and once you find the flow of your poem, it's easy to find where a line might have too many syllables or feel too long. Each poem is different, but once you get to know your poem and work with it a bit, you know what you need to change.

Q: Do you have advice for other young poets?

A: Writing short, fun poems is a good way to start, but if you really want to touch a reader, you have to choose something that connects with you. Trust your readers. And trust yourself, too. You're going to be the hardest editor on your own work. If you feel like a line should go somewhere, put the line there. It's your line; it's your vision. The poem belongs to you. There's no right or wrong in poetry.

Q: What do you like to read?

A: Fantasy, like *Six of Crows* and *Throne of Glass*. And the feel-good books, which my friends tease me for. But I still love them, books like *Infinite in Between* and *Wonder*.

Q: Were you worried about revising with a mentor?

A: I had to get used to the idea of someone else reading my poem. My one concern was that I was going to lose the poem, in a sense, that it wouldn't be my poem anymore. I thought it might feel like a poem I had helped on, but not necessarily my own poem.

It was nice because you know that your mentor is there to help you with your poem, to make it more of the vision you had in the beginning.

Q: How do you know when someone's help is actually helping?

A: You get a more clear vision of what your poem was to begin with, or what you wanted it to be. If someone doesn't ask if you want to change something, but they start suggesting, or saying, "You should definitely change this," they might be trying to make your poem into their poem.

Storm

by

Toby Jacob

What if I am done?
What if I don't want this any more?
I am done being
Shoved,
Hurt and,
Put down,
Because of you.
I don't want to do this!
This dance.
The whirlwind that lifts you up and
Shoves me
Down.
With your words like the thunder on the horizon
I feel every word
Every jab.
I have to stand by myself
I have to stand alone and suffer
I hope for freedom,

Storm

I hope for this to end,
For the raining skies to part
Then the eye of the storm passes over me,
I think I am free
But everywhere I go,
There you are.
You are my shadow,
My unwanted mirror,
The storm might return and then,
If I were to break like
My grandmother's glass elephant,
Then all my cracks would show,
And the stable world I live in would be turned
Upside-down like a snow globe.
I would shatter at the seams
And no one would pick up my pieces
But if I were to break, maybe you would leave,
Then I would be free
I would smile.
I would say how lucky I am.
I would be broken but free
And isn't that better than whole and ensnared?
I would know that you were gone and I could sleep easy again.
But like the storm on the horizon, you would lurk, ready.
Waiting for my fear to return,
Your words like sleet and ice
Pierce my thin shield.
I don't know how long until it cracks.
But every day I face that fear of unraveling at the seams,
That my little boat will capsize in your stormy sea.
I am scared and
No one seems to hear me.

I don't know if I can take this
With every crash of your words
I am pushed farther into the hole
That will never end.
They say it gets better
That the storm can't last forever
But what if the storm is immortal
This neverending dance
I thought that if I were
Kind
Caring
And empathetic
You would leave,
But the storm finds me.
The only way to avoid it is to go unnoticed
I crave that,
To be unnoticed
But my roots are too deep,
The wind ripping at my branches and leaves,
Thrashing against my trunk,
I cannot disappear like I used to be able to.
I wonder,
Will I ever be the same?
Or will I always live in
Fear of you?

Building to a Climax

Ernesto Cisneros guided Oliver Jackson through a revision focused on building suspense in Oliver's story, "Piece by Piece."

Dear Reader,

Coming up with unique and surprising ending for a story is something many authors set out to do, but it is no easy task. Yet, in his story, "Piece by Piece," Oliver manages to do exactly that.

One of the things that Oliver and I wanted to do during the revision process was try and build up the suspense in a way that would make his climactic moment really stand out.

Part of Oliver's hard work was making his main character's journey into madness a bit more gradual. This allows the reader to witness the transformation taking place.

> *I'm hungry*, the man thought as he continued through Hornshaw. *I better get back home quickly so I can get a bite to eat.*
>
> "Why not try that bakery you passed?" said a voice in his head. "The bread is free, yours for the taking."

In this brief excerpt, we see the moment in which the voice in the thief's head transitions into an actual voice, becoming a character in itself. However, Oliver did not simply clean up his plot. He also added backstory to his character that enforces the thief's madness—a very important detail that helps drive the story forward.

To help him do this, Oliver used a technique that requires a bit of time and commitment. Oliver wanted to make sure that he was relating the information in the best possible way and to ensure this, he took the time and effort to rewrite the beginning to his story from a completely new perspective: first person point of view. While the actual words never made it to the final version, the information that he got did.

In the end, what helped transform Oliver's story was his willingness (and eagerness) to revise. Remember, talent is never measured by one's first draft. It is measured by the final version.

Happy writing,
Ernesto Cisneros

Ernesto Cisneros was born in the gang-ridden and often marginalized part of Santa Ana. By adolescence, he began questioning his place in the world. In his senior year in high school, he discovered a love of literature that continued to grow. However, it was not until he began teaching kids with similar backgrounds to himself that he learned about the value and need for literary diversity. And that is when he began writing books for children. He believes in creating realistic (often flawed) characters with everyday struggles. His book, *The Writing on the Wall*, is the fictional but very personal story of his life growing up on Santa Ana. Learn more about Ernesto's work at *www.ernestocisneros.com*.

Oliver Jackson

Oliver is currently an eighth grader at Newark Junior High School. In between books, he enjoys camping, hiking, and just hanging out with his family. He is aspiring to become a Senior Boy Scout Leader and hopes to someday write professionally, or simply for fun. Oliver has written numerous other stories for the Young Authors program at his school. He also has a dog named Scout, a fabulous frisky golden retriever with poisonous breath and big fangs.

Ernesto Cisneros: What changed when you revised and focused on building to the climax of your story?

Oliver Jackson: The main change after my revisions was that there was a better and refined buildup of insanity in the main character. This included the paragraph where he really loses it.

Q: What did you think of the revision process?

A: I have never worked with someone else to revise one of my stories as I have with this contest, and I liked the process of revising. I think that it really helped my story flow, and make sense, along with other improvements.

Q: When did you start writing?

A: I started writing in Kindergarten with my epic novel, *The Red*

Motorcycle, but really got into writing in fourth grade, with my discovery of the books designed for older readers. These stories made me want to write like they were written.

Q: What are your favorite books?
A: My favorite books are in the Inheritance series by Christopher Paolini, and almost all of Edgar Allan Poe's short stories.

Q: What advice do you have for writers who are revising their work?
A: Advice to writers revising their work: keep an open mind, no change has to be permanent, all ideas are just that–ideas–and anything could change in your book. But, I would tell them to keep some part of their writing the same, to go with their gut, especially if it sounds like they want it to.

Piece by Piece

by

Oliver Jackson

I dedicate this story to Edgar Allan Poe, whose style is one I used writing this story, whose stories have captivated me and changed my preference in reading and my style of writing forever.

A man walked through the dark streets of Hornshaw, England, his stomach groaning painfully, looking for something to eat. *I'll just go into the bakery and get some bread*, the man thought to himself. *Just fine to hold me over until I can get a meal.* The man then realized the bakery had been long closed. He hesitated before thinking, *I'll just have to wait until I get home*, but really, in the war-torn battleground that was his mind, his conscience and his inner thief were struggling for control. The man briskly walked around a corner into the stiff blackness of the night.

I'm hungry, the man thought as he continued through Hornshaw. *I better get back home quickly so I can get a bite to eat.*

"Why not try that bakery you passed," said a voice in his head.

"The bread is free, yours for the taking."

So he turned and strolled into the bakery's courtyard, bending his skinny frame under the nearly seven-foot arch of the entrance.

"Wait," he said to the voice. "Why should I steal from these hardworking souls when I have plenty of food at home?"

"You shall," said the voice, "for it benefits you and it is easy—so easy, for all you have to do is go and take it, and the thought of it will trouble you no more."

So the man fell victim to the voice and took the bread, sprinting all the way home, immense guilt plaguing his thoughts.

The next morning, the thief awoke and felt a hunger. Not as you would feel if you required sustenance, but as though you must fulfill a need, a need for something, and that something the thief could not discern. He thought to himself, *How peculiar. What is this feeling?* for he had not felt this for many years. As he was making breakfast, he tore a chunk from a loaf of bread, and suddenly blacked out . . .

As a seven-year-old, I was riding from my friend's house. "I love the doll that she has," I remember thinking. "I wonder if she would notice if I took it."

Immediately, I rejected the idea, knowing she would notice if it went missing, and wondered how I could sneak it out without being seen.

"You might take it piece by piece," came a surprisingly clear thought, "so that eventually you would have all of it."

So I did. I first took the arms, severing them with sharp sticks, hiding the rest of the doll under a loose floorboard. Then the next day, I took the legs, twisting them until they popped off. The next time I visited my friend, I ripped the stomach in two, the puffs of cotton spilling everywhere. Lastly, I wrenched the head from the dismembered carcass. When I finally had all of it, I did not feel joy; instead, I felt emptiness.

After he had regained consciousness, he felt strange pangs as he went about his daily tasks, cleaning his garments, washing his cutlery and dishes, and brushing the dust off of his prized possessions. The feeling even persisted through his lunch, a hearty meal of mutton and spuds, and into his daily walk. A strange thing happened during his walk: the feeling grew unbearable, but this was with good reason, soon to be presented to him.

"Curses," he gasped, as he leaned on a wall for support. "Why these terrible pains?"

An aged lady hobbled towards him, concerned, and it was then that the feeling showed itself. It was greed, an overwhelming greed that enveloped his whole being, wrapping itself around his conscience, blocking out the good in him, rendering his lawful parts useless in face of the voice, an all too familiar voice. Before he was completely taken over, the thief tried to fight it with every grain of his being, but it was to no avail, and he soon succumbed to the voice.

The elderly woman was reaching towards him, but when he collapsed, she became disconcerted and took a shaky step backwards. The voice, as if from very far away, began speaking.

"What a nice jeweled cane she has, I'd very much like that." The thief fought, but his fighting was without heart, for he knew there was no use. The thief, or rather the voice, snatched the cane from her, and she collapsed to the ground, weak without it. Even when he regained control of his body, he did not help the old lady, nor give her the cane back.

This time the thief spoke. "It is nice having this expensive cane; why not keep it?"

The voice had no quarrel with that. The thief ran off.

The thief awoke, tired from the stressful night before. He thought of how he had flitted from building to building, terrified that someone would catch him and put him away, or worse. When he had returned, he had hidden the cane in his cellar, away from the eyes of any that might accuse him. When he awoke, he did not ponder the subject any longer.

"Why worry about something that is already done?" he mumbled to himself, and he moved on with his day.

But the next day, again something happened during his walk: a terrible urge that he could not ignore. So once more he stole.

Sadly, this was not the end of it. All week the thief positively needed to steal, just to keep the hunger away—and the voice quiet— if just for a precious moment. But the voice would not be silenced.

One day, the thief was lurching and pacing around his room feverishly shaking his hands and shouting, "Oh, the pleasure of stealing! The amazing sensation of taking what should already be mine! How I love the sweet smell of the night air as I break through windows and doors, every step bringing me closer to satisfying the terrible need to take."

The thief jerked to a halt, barely able to still his twitching hands, grasping at the air, as though snatching his precious treasures.

He continued, "Oh, I feel as if I might burst from the pressure of it! I must go, my terrible hunger allows me no time, no enjoyment of life. I feel no feeling but want, I have no urge but to take, no . . ." The thief never finished his ranting.

The voice took over, commanding, "Yes! Yes! Now go! Take!" With that, the thief crashed down the stairs and into the still, quiet night.

At the week's closing, the thief was stealing constantly, and made no effort to resist the voice. Stealing had become a habit for him, an addiction, and he could not stop. The thief started to become reckless: looting rich homes, and even guarded museums, to sate his hunger. This was when the thief's spree came to an end. He was caught. He was locked in a cell, doomed to stay until the end of his days.

On the second night after his jailing, he heard a voice. An all too familiar voice that made his heart stop and his blood freeze. The voice of greed, his greed, and he could not escape it. He sat, helpless, in his cell waiting to see what the voice made of him.

"What a pretty doll they have here," it said. "I would like to have it. I will just take it. But no, they would surely notice, I will just have to take it piece by piece . . ."

Interiority

Kristi Wright mentored Shannon Ma through a revision focused on a character's interior feelings and reactions in Shannon's poem, "Beautiful Sounds."

Dear Reader,

In "Beautiful Sounds," Shannon Ma crafted a wonderful personal narrative that has both universal significance and emotional resonance. We all can relate to what it's like to compete for something that we care deeply about, but then feel as if we didn't do our best.

For Shannon's revision, we focused on interiority. Interiority is a big word that basically means a character's thoughts, emotions, and reactions to the situation at hand. You accomplish interiority by dipping into the character's head at important moments. Interiority is emotional "telling," but not the simple telling of emotions, such as "She is sad." It reinforces character feelings or turning points in key moments, and it ensures that an emotional moment really "lands" with the reader.

Shannon already weaved her thoughts, emotions, and reactions into "Beautiful Sounds." However, there were spots throughout where she could add more specific interiority to ensure that her story resonated as much as possible with her reader.

For example, in Shannon's original narrative, the reader is introduced to the main character, whose emotions are "drooping like the petals of the wilting flower." She is both delighted for performing mistake-free and sad because she could have done better. This was very engaging, but we didn't know what she thought could have gone better. Was it her articulation? Her musical phrasing? Or was she just one of those people who always thinks she does the worst?

It turned out that the main character had rushed through her piece, so her pace was off. In her revision, Shannon added the following specific thought: " . . . but today, the utmost ultimate day, I rushed through my Bach concerto after practicing for weeks with a steady tempo." Now we know exactly what went wrong. We don't have to guess.

A good way to find places that might need more interiority is to ask a family member or friend to read your story and mark spots where they weren't sure why a character felt a certain way or acted a certain way. Those spots are excellent candidates for adding more thoughts and reactions (interiority).

I hope this concept of interiority resonates with you. Play with it in your own stories. When you give your readers insight into a character's thoughts, emotions, and reactions to the situation at hand, you give them the opportunity to connect with that character in a deeply personal way.

Happy writing,
Kristi Wright

Kristi Wright is the Assistant Regional Advisor for the San Francisco/South region of the Society of Children's Book Writers and Illustrators. She offers writing workshops at the elementary school level with a focus on point of view and sensory detail. She is also the assistant editor for a blog that analyzes middle grade novels as mentor texts for writers: *www.mglunchbreak.com*. Her indie-published futuristic middle grade adventure series, *The Basker Twins in the 31st Century*, raises funds and awareness for a rare, childhood-onset disease, Friedreich's ataxia. Find her at *www.kristiwrightauthor.com* and on Twitter @KristiWrite.

Shannon Ma

Shannon is eleven years old and heading into seventh grade at Redwood Middle School. She lives with her parents and little sister in Saratoga, California. She has loved to play the violin since she was three, and she also loves dancing. She is a fan of fantasy and enjoys writing fanfiction Harry Potter comedy scripts whenever she has the chance. When Shannon was in fourth grade, she published her first book, *My Dream Will Come True*, a collection of her art and writing from kindergarten to fourth grade. Shannon also writes in her online blog in her free time, where she keeps a daily record of her thoughts, scripts, narratives, and more. Her favorite color is light green, followed closely by light purple and light blue. If she could visit anywhere in the world, she'd visit Paris, France.

Kristi Wright: What inspired you to write "Beautiful Sounds"?
Shannon Ma: I competed in the musical competition I wrote about in my story when I was seven years old and then again when I was nine. This was a true story, and it was a time when I grew a lot so I decided that it would be a good story to use for this writing competition.

Q: Was it hard to write a narrative about yourself?
A: Not really. I actually had a fresh memory of it. I could remember it because that day was one of the most memorable days I've ever had.

Q: What changed in your story when you added interiority?
A: I thought the story was much clearer. You know how when you add interiority, it's supposed to help the reader understand the character better? I felt like when I added the thoughts, it also made me understand myself better.

Q: Did you learn anything from this revision process that you can use as you write your next story?
A: Yes, I can. When I write future narratives, I can add in more interiority. It makes a better story.

Q: Do you like to revise?
A: I do like revising my work. I can always find a place that I can improve. I also like when another person reads my work and gives me suggestions.

Q: What's your favorite part of "Beautiful Sounds"?
A: My favorite part is my emotional explosion when I was with my mom. At that time, I really got the rock out of my heart.

Q: What advice would you give other writers about revision?
A: I would tell them that, no matter what, you can always improve a story. I would recommend using figurative language because it helps describe.

Q: Are you writing anything right now?
A: Yes, I'm a Harry Potter fan. I like to make up scripts for the characters. Mostly I write scripts where the characters insult each other—Harry, Ron, Hermione and Malfoy, sometimes Snape.

Beautiful Sounds

by

Shannon Ma

I trudged out of the music room with my violin. I felt like a sad, wilting flower—I had my angelic white dress on and gelled hair, and sparkling silver shoes that completed my outfit, but my emotions were drooping like the petals of the wilting flower. I wanted to barge into the music room and ask the judges for a second chance to perform, but that would not be the smartest choice. I simultaneously felt delighted for finishing a performance free of mistakes, but also sad. I practiced so hard on the violin the past several days, but today, the utmost ultimate day, I rushed through my Bach concerto after practicing for weeks with a steady tempo.

Think happy, think happy, THINK HAPPY!! I told myself as I stepped out of the music hall in Stanford. I saw my mom waiting for me, where she had been while I was performing.

"Hi, Shannon!" she exclaimed, looking glad to see me, and I felt a knot in my stomach. Then she asked the question that was the last thing I wanted to hear. "How was your performance?"

I glowered and lowered my eyes, pretending to examine the ground, but quickly smiled a large, happy smile and said, "It was *awesome*!" I injected as much confidence and enthusiasm as I could into my voice, but Mom looked worried.

"Are you okay?" she asked.

"Mom," I said. "It was *the best*. I never lie, and I can't imagine why you wouldn't believe so!"

Nobody would understand if I even attempted to explain how terribly I performed, and talking at all felt as if it were draining every last drop of energy I had.

"I believe you, and of *course* you always do really well!" Mom said, and put her arm around my shoulder as we walked to the car.

On the way home, my dad, my clueless little sister, and my mom were chatting away happily, but gradually quieted down as they saw how mute I was. We drove back home, passing through grassy parks with playgrounds, tall buildings, and a multitude of houses through the city of Palo Alto. I used my mom's iPhone to take pictures of the view at the car window, and for some odd reason, I edited them all to black and white.

The car screeched to a halt and we were finally home.

I stormed into the house and down the hallway into my room, hopping onto my bed. My stress and frustration were like irritating mosquitoes that wouldn't fly away. I tried to calm down, but it didn't help that I felt like I was on the verge of tears whenever I looked at my violin case, and especially when I looked at the shiny first-place trophy I won in the past at the same violin competition.

Dinner was most uneventful. Though the television was on and quiet chatter was going on, I was in my own island and my mind was shut down. Mom glanced at me every once in a while, looking quite concerned, as if expecting me to explode out of my seat–but she kept quiet.

After dinner, Mom followed me to my room and sat down beside me on my bed.

"Shannon," Mom said gently. "It's just a competition . . . "

Before she finished, I burst into a flood of tears.

"I just *really want to win*!" I exclaimed.

All the bitter and resentful thoughts I had earlier were gushing out. I was angry at myself, at fate, at the world, at the universe. *Why* did I rush? A mad chorus of *"Why?"* accompanied with furious, regretful thoughts, rang in my head.

"*I did terrible*!" I yelled this time, without realizing what I was saying. "*I could have done better.*"

Misery and dread were like boulders sitting on top of me. I wiped my tears with my sleeve.

"It doesn't matter if you win or lose," Mom said.

"I know! I never *just* want to win!" I said, then paused. "But I still really want to win."

We shared several seconds of silence, where Mom pondered and I despaired.

"Did you try your best?" Mom asked.

"Yes!! I tried all I could! You know how much I love those pieces!"

I loved my Bach concerto. I loved making music. I loved every drop of sweat, every callus on my fingertips from the months of hard work. But my performance was something I had to accept.

More silence.

"Then you won!" Mom said.

We embraced each other and a rock was lifted from my heart. Someone understood. The world wasn't going to end. Replacing the rock was a sense of inner peace that flooded through my mind and heart. *Win or lose*, I thought, *this will stay with me forever.* I could tell Mom felt the same way.

I sniffed my stuffy nose loudly. In that hug, all our sorrows and woe were squeezed out like a sponge spouting out water, and for a moment the room was full of quiet love.

The next day, as usual, I picked up my beautiful, golden-crimson instrument and played violin. As I looked at my fingers flying on the fingerboard, I felt my heart flying along with the music. I remembered all the poems I wrote about my instrument, and I just realized that I really, truly loved to play violin.

This is what violin is supposed to be about: cherishing the music with all your heart, not marching home with a gleaming golden trophy proudly declaring "First Place."

A week later . . .

I was stretched out cozily on my bed, grinning from ear to ear as I softly hummed along with the lively music coming from a Bach recording of Hilary Hahn, a remarkable violinist who never participated in a single violin competition.

"Shannon?" Mom and Dad poked their heads into my room.

"You won second place in the violin competition. Awesome job!"

"That's great! Thanks!" I exclaimed.

I turned back to listen to Hilary Hahn's music. The elegant and graceful sound that came out of her violin filled my heart with pure bliss, and for a moment I was in my own world, just the music and me.

That's me, I thought. *This is my future. Lovely music and beautiful sounds from my heart.*

Rhythm

Jena Brigantino and Camille Chu worked together to bring out the natural rhythm in Camille's poem, "So Many Heroines."

Dear Reader,

Poetry can be difficult to revise sometimes. Poets like Camille, who write poetry in rhyme, already spent a lot of time choosing the "just right" rhyming words. Camille's rhythm flowed well and was very balanced from one line to another. Rhythm is especially important in rhyming poetry.

We chose to explore rhythm a little more as a revision focus. Sometimes as poets we know exactly how our poem should sound, but when we hear someone else read our work, it doesn't sound right. I read Camille's poem aloud to her so she could hear how it sounds. I asked her to pay attention to pauses and stumbles. I also asked Camille to ask a friend or two to read her poem aloud. Camille discovered a few places in her poem that weren't sounding right. Camille ended up getting rid of a few words and shortening a three-syllable word to a two-syllable word in order to balance out the rhythm. These small revisions polished the poem wonderfully!

When revising a poem, remember, your original piece will always be there, so trying new options can't hurt. You may always decide that you want to keep the first words you chose. By playing with different options, you become even more confident in your choices.

Jena Brigantino

Jena Brigantino grew up playing outdoors in central California, where she dreamed up stories featuring animals. Jena wishes she had the opportunity to experience an Inklings program as a child. She strives to extend the opportunity to as many children as possible as Managing Director of Society of Young Inklings. She holds a BA in creative arts and a minor in education from San José State University.

Camille Chu

Camille is in second grade. She loves to travel and her second favorite way to see the world is to read. She enjoys all types of fiction and adventure books. She also likes music, swimming, and gymnastics.

Jena Brigantino: When did you start writing?
Camille Chu: I have been keeping a journal since I was four years old.

Q: How do you come up with your ideas?
A: From books I read or places I have visited.

Q: How do you feel about the revisions you made in your story?
A: The revisions were very useful!

Q: In the end, you changed a few words of your poem after you played with ideas. What do you think of the finished poem now?
A: I like the finished poem better now.

Q: What advice do you have for other Inklings who don't like revision very much?
A: Try it out—if you don't like it you can always change it back.

So Many Heroines

by

Camille Chu

My favorite heroines are brilliant and kind
with curious, magical, and mischievous minds.
Please come meet them as they are quite a find!

Violet Baudelaire is very clever
Using her own inventions she learns how to sever
Ties with a series of unfortunate events to make things better!

Mary Lennox and Gilly Hopkins start as spoiled brats
But after finding a secret garden and a family, they learn that
The world is actually full of love, not spats!

Annika von Tannenberg and Theodora Tenpenny are curious and
brave
While figuring out their families' mysterious pasts, they save

the priceless star of Kazan and a painting from under an egg!

Martine Allen and Odge the Ogre have magical powers
To rescue the last white giraffe from poachers whose nature is sour
And a prince by using the secret of platform 13 before the final
hour!

But my favorite heroine is Anne Shirley with a house whose gables
are green
She means well, but gets in so much trouble it makes you scream
And laugh because Anne is so funny and keen!

From all of them I now know
To be a heroine you don't have to have riches or a beautiful glow
But you have to have brains and a heart that can grow!

My favorite heroines come from my beloved books
Open one, join me, and take a look
With these new friends you will get inspired and hooked!

Internal Monologue

Jenn Castro mentored Claire Lignore through a revision focused on the protagonist's thoughts in Claire's story, "Orphaned by Dancing Red."

Dear Reader,

If you have challenged yourself to write internal monologue in a story, feel proud! But how do you know when you have enough internal monologue so the story maintains the same feel and rhythm throughout the narrative? Claire Lignore's "Orphaned by Dancing Red" impressed our team of readers immediately because of Claire's ability to enter the minds of her characters and create believable internal monologue. When Claire and I met to revise her story, there was little that needed changing. However, we wondered if, because Claire was so adept at writing from the animal's perspective, she might be able to use this ability to create even more internal monologue throughout the narrative.

First, we brainstormed the places where Claire could make additions. One spot was at the end, which—because it takes place ten years after the fire—at first Claire had written as a summary. Interestingly, we both saw that this section would be even stronger if Claire could revise it and, using more internal monologue, tie it seamlessly to the earlier story. Then, using her research about orangutans, Claire brainstormed several ideas that Merdeka, her main character, could "say." Claire considered adding dialogue for Martabat, Merdeka's baby, but in the end wisely assigned the dialogue to Merdeka.

Claire did important work that all writers must do in revision. First, she brainstormed several ideas and places she could use them. Second, she considered all the moments in her story she could change. Claire kept in close contact with me throughout her revision process. I was impressed with her enthusiasm and nearly daily writing throughout the revision period. Even though Claire consulted with me about her changes and the places to put them, she always made the final decisions. It was fun to watch her make choices about where and how she'd add more dialogue.

If you're writing a story, you might try Claire's revision approach. Read over your story with someone else, and look for places you could change. If, like Claire, you've done research for your story, revisit it, so you can build those details into your character's thoughts and feelings.

Before making final changes, look again at your story to make sure the additions are needed and make your story even stronger. Read the story not as a writer, but as a reader. Do your newly added character thoughts fit? Do they enhance the character? You will know because you will feel what you want your reader to feel! Claire found the best places to include more internal dialogue. Like Claire, you may add only a few sentences. Letting those changes enliven your character, and tying the dialogue at the beginning of the story to the words at the end, can enhance your story and make it more how you want it to be.

Like Claire advises, be careful about your choices, but have fun revising!

Jenn Castro

Jenn Castro is the author of *Mom Me*, a children's picture book about a kid who only wants to play with Mom. Jenn has always written—on napkins, backs of envelopes, and in newspapers, diaries, and journals. Jenn loves any kind of children's book, especially coming-of-age stories and middle grade chapter books about ordinary young people. In addition to children's books, Jenn also writes about parenting, stop signs, and other quirky parts of life as a guest blogger and on her website, *jenncastro.com*. A Young Inklings mentor and teacher, Jenn lives in California with her husband and two kids.

Claire Lignore

Claire just finished the fifth grade at Duniway Elementary in Portland, Oregon. Beyond writing, she loves nature, hiking, adventure, and hanging out with family and friends. She also runs cross country and plays basketball. In her spare time, she sets up fundraisers and raises awareness about endangered animals with a conservation group she started called Together We Defend Nature. When Claire grows up, she hopes to become a primatologist, and travel the world, writing books to inspire people to respect the Earth. She's proud to be a vegetarian. Her favorite animal is an orangutan, because they are intelligent, peaceful, and strong.

Jenn Castro: How did you revise "Dancing Red" to include more internal monologue from Merdeka?

Claire Lignore: It was not difficult. I used my research about the orangutan. In one place, I remembered the mommy likes to cover her baby in leaves and added that. I tried to have fun with the revisions. I didn't want to make too many changes, and I was careful to not make the story too long.

Q: What advice do you have for Inklings who are revising so their story doesn't change too much from the original idea?

A: Keep reading the story over and over and decide if making a change will help the story.

Q: What do you like about writing?

A: I enjoy making up characters and bringing together different characters and story ideas.

Q: Where do you like to write?

A: I write in my room and in the living room. I like to write when my family is around me. I enjoy the sound of their talking in the background. I like listening to their conversations while I'm writing.

Q: Who do you share your stories with?

A: I share my stories with my family. I read my stories to them to get ideas and suggestions. For "Dancing Red," I asked them to make sure the story was from Merdeka's perspective.

Q: Do you ever get blocked? What do you do?

A: I go back to my notebook and reread the story. If I am writing a longer story, I sometimes lose interest. If I get tired of the story, I start a new one. If I haven't written for a while, sometimes I'm not sure what to write and I don't have any story ideas. If that happens, I wait till I get more story ideas or I look at a story I wrote a long time ago and write more about that story.

Q: Are you working on another story?

A: I'm writing a story about a world broken into two groups: the luckies, who have everything, and the unluckies who are in the rest of the world. In my story, a character from the unluckies meets one of the luckies.

Orphaned by Dancing Red

by

Claire Lignore

Merdeka's my name; it means *free* in Indonesian. Merdeka is the name Mommy gave to me because she said I was *meant* to be free. But that all changed after the raging dancing red swept over my home. Mine and Mommy's. I thought the Sumatran forest was just for Mommy and me. I didn't know there were more of us.

This is the story of me. Me, Merdeka. It all started in a forest. A forest with green trees and a safe place to sleep, and Mom. I *love* my Mommy. I would cling to her belly while she swung from branch to branch. She shared her favorite foods with me and she told me which foods were *not* good to eat.

Mommy taught me how to use a stick when there was fruit with a hard shell. At first, I couldn't crack it, but I did because Mommy taught me. She showed me how to find white six legged wigglers that eat dead leaves without getting stung, and she taught me how to catch the little fur balls for a tasty treat every once in a while.

At night, and a big portion of the day, I slept in the treetops in

a nest of leaves and twigs. It was snug up there, and warm. Everything was good. At *least* for a while.

I was four years old when it happened. Not *all* at once. It happened slowly. The more trees that the dancing red ate, the more scary it was.

Mommy and I were chomping on my favorite fruit (durians). I was getting good at cracking the shell and eating the insides. The fruit tasted marvelous. I can still remember its yummy filling. I could hear the peaceful sound of the wind brushing the trees, gently. The birds were chirping loud and clear.

But, suddenly, I heard the most unusual sound. It was a yelp. A yelp of a Sumatran tiger. I was scared of those beasts because sometimes they ate orangutan babies. But I wasn't scared of them today. This time, I felt bad for it. What was happening? A call rang out in the woods. It was a call of a young elephant. It sounded hurt. I looked up to Mom. She hugged me and bent down to kiss me.

I lifted my head out of Mommy's grasp and I saw dancing red. It jumped and howled all around me. Its breath made me choke. Mom started to run through the trees, faster and faster. I held on tight.

My eyes burned, and my throat felt like it was being stung from the inside. Mommy's hand was on my body making sure I wouldn't fall off. Her other hand was pushing branches out of the way. I could still hear the cries of the elephants in the distance. Something bad was happening.

The dancing red moved so fast. I felt terribly hot. Mommy gracefully and with speed swung to the next tree. The dancing red made a popping sound and swept through my home. Trees were falling down all around us. What would happen when the dancing red came to us? Mommy was losing her breath. *Go faster*, I thought, *please?*

A branch ripped into Mommy's red fur. She slowed down. There was blood. I looked away. But something pulled my eyes back. It was a branch of thorns. It gashed into her shoulder. Mommy screeched. I couldn't make a sound. When the dancing red came to me, all I could do was wait.

When I opened my eyes, I saw a creature above me. It had fur on top of its head, like the fur on mine, except it didn't have any *other* fur. *Instead* of fur, the rest of its body was covered with blue and green, like the moss on trees. Was I imagining things? Was I dead? Where's Mommy? And what are these creatures?

Just then, I heard a few weird sounding grunts. I had never heard such strange sounds. I couldn't figure them out. It was like many voices at once; an elephant's trumpet, a rhino's bellow, and a tiger's roar.

"You're safe now, buddy. You're at the wild animal vet center— you're safe now." I had no clue what that meant.

I looked at my surroundings but I wasn't really looking, I was staring. Staring hard and angry. Where's Mommy? I need her. Then everything came back to me. Was Mommy dead? No, I thought. No! Did the dancing red swallow her? Mommy was just getting food, probably.

A wave of pain went through my arm. It was like it was being stung over and over again. I felt like biting the creature above me. As

hard as possible. Stop thinking that, I told myself. Why would I want to hurt this creature?

I went to sleep again, and this time when I woke up, I was being held. Have I been here before? The place wasn't familiar so it must have been dangerous. I looked at my arm. My fur was gone. What happened to me? I tried to suck in the memory of eating durians with Mommy. I would give anything to be back home.

"Her burns are getting better," the creature above me grunted again. It was driving me crazy not understanding them. There were lots of animals in my forest who I couldn't understand but these, well, their language was the strangest of all. The oddest thing about them was they didn't have much fur! At first, I was sure they were like me. But that was because I was dizzy and my eyes weren't seeing clearly.

Also, I couldn't get the thought out of my mind that they might eat me.

The creature grunted again, "I know it hurts, little guy. I can't believe anyone would burn a forest for darn old palm oil. I'm so sorry they killed your mother."

They didn't just grunt. Sometimes they cooed like a bird or bellowed like a rhino, or even whined like a cloud of mosquitoes when they had their backs to me. Were they saying I'd make a delicious meal? I hadn't realized I wasn't resting in a nest. I was in something else, something white and soft, like the wings of a flycatcher. My arm hurt when I got up.

"Easy on it, girl. We just treated your burns while you were asleep," one of them said in its strange language.

The place was weird, the color of clouds. It made me uncomfortable. Was this where I would be eaten?

"I know what your name should be," cooed the creature. "Harry." What was it saying? It sounded excited. Maybe they weren't going to eat me after all!

"You okay, Harry?"

They called me that so much, it almost felt like my name. But I'm Merdeka, right? I'm supposed to be free.

I decided that it had been too long and they would not eat me. Maybe they're nice creatures and Mommy would be back soon?

I stayed there for a day longer. It wasn't quite as scary anymore. I still would definitely prefer to be with Mommy right now. Why couldn't I just go home? Hopefully Mommy was looking for me. If I spoke the creature's language, I would tell them: "My name's Merdeka, not Harry or whatever you're calling me."

A creature with long fur that came out of its head checked on me.

"She's doing great," it grunted. "Bring her to the rehab center."

I wanted to learn a few words of their language. Hopefully, when Mommy came back we could learn it together.

I was once again tired and took a nap. This time when I woke up, I was in a place with black tree branches arranged in a weird way in front of me. It was like the creatures had built a nest all around me with no way out. What was this place? It reminded me of the time when I was stuck in a hollowed-out tree. I banged on the tree branches, but they wouldn't budge. I was furious, so I banged some more, but it still wouldn't budge!

"You'll be out of the cage soon," a creature grunted.

I looked around. There were other orangutans wrapped in black tree branches. I searched carefully for my mother, but she

was not there. It was stuffy and hot. I jumped up and down. The orangutans around me were either asleep or looking curious. One of the orangutans was about my age and the rest were grown-ups. I looked at all the other orangutans and wondered, Why were they here? Why was I here?

Suddenly, we stopped. I lurched forward in my little nest and banged my head on one of the branches. *Ouch! That hurt!* It was harder than any tree I'd ever felt.

"We're here!" a creature grunted.

Forest was all around me. Like my home. My wondrous home. But where was Mommy? Did the dancing red eat her? Was she swallowed by the *mean* dancing red?

But instead of being let go in the forest, I was sent to another place with more tough tree branches. Luckily, it was bigger and it even had a tree in the middle of it. I was let go into this place, all to myself. At least for a few hours.

Then another orangutan, maybe one year older than me, came. I was disappointed because I didn't have it all to myself anymore. I admit, I was also a little relieved. Finally, I wasn't alone. Maybe this orangutan would be like Mommy.

Me and that orangutan became good friends. She understood me and I understood her. It was the perfect match. Every day, the creatures would take us out in the real forest and watch us swing from tree to tree, eat fruit, leaves, and insects. It became a routine. Our friendship grew stronger and stronger. Durian, that is her name, had almost the exact story as me.

One day, a creature came in. It was holding something that looked like another arm, with a big hand at the bottom.

"Well, I better clean your enclosure, Harry and May." That was what they called Durian. The creature started to scrape the ground, lifting up our poop. I walked over curiously. The creature stopped scraping the ground. I carefully took the weird tool out of the creature's hands, and started to scrape the ground myself, copying the exact movements the creature had made. Scrape, lift, scrape, lift.

The creature looked at me with amusement in its eyes, and then started to make a high pitched sound—ha ha ha—that frightened me. What was it trying to tell me? It sounded a bit like when in my home, Mommy made a high pitched shrieking sound when it was about to rain hard. Then she would cover my head with a giant leaf. I dropped the tool and ran away. That night I practiced making the high-pitched sound.

Every day, I grew healthier and happier and so did Durian. My arm was almost healed and I was feeling much better. Durian told me that she got her name because she always threw a fit if her mother didn't give her durians for every meal.

I longed for my mother each night. I wondered if Durian did, too. I imagined grabbing on to Mommy's chest and splashing water on her. That couldn't happen anymore. It would never happen again.

When it was time to eat, the creatures took us to the trees and watched us eat leaves, insects, and fruit. I liked to look at them and listen to their funny language and ways. Sometimes they ate from something that looked like a turtle's shell with two sticks. Their food couldn't have been six-legged white wigglers though. If so, the wigglers must've been dead. It was very interesting to watch them.

Two of the grunts—"*rehab center*"—that I learned from the creatures I found to mean *my home*. I was getting to like my new life,

but still, every night and day, I missed Mommy.

One day, I felt like something different might happen. I felt like something was about to change. Me and Durian went into the forest to find food like usual, but I sensed we were staying out there too long. The creatures taking care of us motioned us away. I didn't know what was happening.

"Go. You're free, Harry and May," the creatures grunted.

What are they telling us to do? But deep inside, I knew what Durian and I were supposed to do.

That day, we ate and ate but still the creatures didn't call us. We started to get tired of munching on leaves and white wigglers. I rubbed my belly. Suddenly, Durian nudged me. I looked at her, and she looked at me. We both knew exactly what we were supposed to do. I turned back for a moment, and stared at the creatures and the rehab center I was leaving behind, then off we went through the trees. *Will we ever see them again?*

Ten years later . . .

Durian and I started our own families. I have a baby daughter! Nothing could be better!

I still see Durian sometimes. We meet at the creek—with Durian's daughter, Lapar—where we wash ourselves and our kids. An ebony tree leans over the creek. It covers us from the hot sun. I give Durian a knowing smile while we wash our children. They will always be safe in the forest. At least that's what I hope.

My baby is adorable. She's gorgeous. She has knotty red fur and a happy face. I am so proud of my four-year-old. We swing down from the trees, and to the creek, where she splashes me until I'm soaked. I always cover my face with my arms, but she keeps splashing anyway. I tell her stories about her grandmother, and what it was like at the rehab center, and she listens. She listens with all her heart. Even though the creatures were nice to me at the rehab center, I don't want my baby ever to have to go there.

When it rains, I cover my baby with the leaves of a kapok tree. I make a nest around her.

When I climb to the top of the trees, sometimes I can see dancing red hovering over the forest, far into the distance. When I see it, it's like I have millions of white wigglers crawling around in my tummy, getting ready to sting. I think I can hear the dancing red making popping sounds. I can even smell its breath. I hope it never comes too close to us. No creature should ever feel the sting of dancing red, especially my baby. I wonder if my baby thinks about dancing red like I do. I need to teach her how dangerous it is. Does she shudder when she sees it in the distance?

Do you want to know her name? Well, I named her Martabat, after my mother, which means dignity. She makes me proud when she masters something new. She definitely fits her name. We play a game in the trees, where we try to make noises that other animals make. I want Martabat to know that she is not the only creature in the forest, like I thought when I was her age. I want Martabat to know about the weird creatures that I met. Martabat mimics me when I make a high pitched ha ha ha sound from deep in my throat, like I learned from the creature at the rehab center. She tries her best to copy me when I make the call of a Sumatran tiger. I wonder what she will learn to do next.

At night, and a big portion of the day, I place her in a nest made of leaves and twigs. I teach her to crack the hard shell of durians. Martabat likes that food as much as me.

I teach her how to eat the small white wigglers, without getting stung. I teach her to catch the little fur balls for a tasty treat every once in a while. I teach her all the things that my mom taught me. Now, I've learned the forest is meant for all creatures, but not to destroy. To respect. My name is Merdeka and I am meant to be free.

Internal Logic

Dear Reader,

You're about to read about a Fruit Apocalypse. From the first read of Dylan Lefever's story, I was hooked. What a hilarious idea! What fantastic characters and plot twists and setting details!

Sometimes when you have a clever idea, such as Dylan's idea for this story, it's difficult to see when pieces of the story don't make sense. To be fair, most of the story is wild and over-the-top, so the questions, "Is this realistic?" or "Is this believable?" aren't very helpful. Dylan wasn't going for realistic or believable.

Still, as we worked on his revision, we discovered that no matter how funny a story may be, it still needs to make sense. The phrase writers use to describe this kind of making sense is internal logic. What this phrase means is that the story has to stick to the rules the writer has created. In Dylan's case, he created a world where fruit can grow to incredible sizes. In this world, fruit can also speak and create evil plans to take over the world.

The trouble is, if you have fruit that is powerful enough to take over the world, why don't they do so, immediately? Dylan had to make choices about what the fruit could and couldn't do, about how the magic worked, and how, ultimately, his human characters could face down these powerful enemies.

I was proud of the way Dylan combed through his story, adding details about how the magic worked. He also made adjustments to the beginning and end of the story to make sure that the events of the story didn't contradict one another. The final piece of the revision—probably the hardest—was figuring out how to show Billy's motivation for facing down this cast of evil fruit. Why would a boy brave such danger? Dylan did a nice job weaving relationships and events to help a reader understand Billy's daring actions. Together, all of these adjustments transformed Dylan's story from a funny series of events into a hilarious story that holds together from the first sentence all the way to the end.

If you're working on a funny story and you find that pieces of it don't make sense, try asking yourself questions similar to the ones Dylan asked himself in this revision. Here are a few that might help:

1. What are the rules of the magic in my story?
2. If those are the rules of the magic, what can't happen the way I've written it?
3. What else might happen that *does* fit with the rules of the magic?

One note about these questions: Sometimes when you start picking apart your story, it's easy to feel worried. What if you can't find a solution that works? If you start feeling anxious, take a deep breath. Remember, *you* are the one who has created this story, and you are fully capable of coming up with a solution. In fact, the best creative ideas come from challenges that seem impossible. Stick with the brainstorming process, consider every angle, and you'll be amazed at the solutions that pop to mind.

Enjoy Dylan's story, and prepare to laugh out loud!

Happy reading,
Naomi Kinsman

Naomi Kinsman is the author of the *From Sadie's Sketchbook* series and the award-winning *Spilled Ink, a Writer's Commonplace Book*. Most recently, Naomi co-authored the *Glimmer Girls* series with recording artist, Natalie Grant. Through a decade of writing and directing plays for young people, and serving as a resident artist in classrooms across the country, Naomi developed Writerly Play, which uses game-based strategies and tools to teach young writers. Naomi also founded Society of Young Inklings. She holds a BA in Theatre Arts from Seattle Pacific University and an MA in Writing for Children and Young Adults from Hamline University.

Dylan Lefever

Dylan is entering sixth grade at Kilgour Elementary. Dylan plays many sports, including basketball, baseball, soccer, football with friends, ice-skating, water-skiing, and snow-skiing. When he isn't playing sports, Dylan likes to climb trees and rocks, look up sports stats, and draw. One of the ways he got to know the characters in this story was to draw them. Dylan is already envisioning the sequels for this book, including *Vegetable Invasion*, *Grain-Storm*, and *Dairy Tsunami*.

Naomi Kinsman: How did you feel about the revision process?

Dylan Lefever: First, you have to be patient because it takes a long time. At first I just sat there, and thought about the questions and how to answer them. Then, once an idea popped into my head, they kept coming. It felt hard, and then it felt like revising paid off and made my story better. I was able to go into the story and add detail, so a reader could see my story in their minds. When I read stories I like to picture what is happening in my mind, like how it would look like in a movie.

Q: What did you change in the story?

A: I added the prologue and I added some scenes to make the story more interesting. If a sentence didn't make sense, I changed it. The end of the story didn't make sense with the beginning, so I changed that, too.

Q: What advice would you give other young writers?

A: For revising, you have to be patient. If you work on your story and pay attention to other people's advice, and make changes, your hard work will pay off. Don't just try to fix your writing on your own. Show it to other people and see how you can make it better.

Q: Where did you get the idea for "Fruit Apocalypse"?

A: At the beginning of the year, I thought of writing about a fruit apocalypse and I started a smaller story. But then, a couple months later, I thought about my idea again and expanded the story into this longer version.

Q: What do you like to read?

A: I like to read adventurous things, like Harry Potter, Percy Jackson, and *The Heroes of Olympus*. Now, I'm reading *The Maze Runner* series. I also like to read sports books.

Fruit Apocalypse

by

Dylan Lefever

Prologue

One day at Midville School, kids started launching food across the room—bananas, apples, oranges, watermelon, eggs, even a big slice of steak.

All the ruckus stopped when the door swung open. Janitor Jerry stood in the doorway. Janitor Jerry was the world's greatest cleaner, but if you made a mess, you were in big trouble.

All the kids had frozen except for Sam and John, who were still throwing their oranges and bananas at each other.

"You two come here. You will be cleaning up this whole mess with me after school," Janitor Jerry said with a loud, serious voice.

Sam and John froze with horror on their faces.

That afternoon, when Sam and John were going to the cafeteria to clean up the mess, they saw Janitor Jerry and Principal Ms. Brown talking out in the hallway. When they walked up, Ms. Brown nodded and walked away.

"So who's ready to clean up?" Janitor Jerry asked with a cheerful voice.

Sam thought he would die of boredom if he had to go in there. The boys had cleaned up half the cafeteria when Janitor Jerry finally said they could they leave.

Chapter One: The Beginning

Janitor Jerry had been sweeping up the final scraps when he turned to see the pieces of an apple coming back together. Then, legs popped out of the apple–and arms. It turned and stared at Janitor Jerry. Janitor Jerry took off running down the hallway, slipping on a banana peel. He looked down and noticed the banana peel had eyes and was squirming around with only one arm.

Janitor Jerry looked back to see the whole hallway filled with bananas, some walking and some on the ground like the first. Janitor Jerry was surrounded by bananas, when a stampede of crazy one-eyed pineapples came through the door. Bananas were getting stepped on until several pineapple feet hit Janitor Jerry in the head. He couldn't believe what was happening. Another foot knocked into his head. He was woozy, but there was something caught on his leg. He looked down to see a purple diamond necklace dangling off his foot. Another foot hit him hard and he fell unconscious–or at least that's what he thought happened. No one ever saw him again and the school closed down. All the kids were transferred to a new school, including Sam and John.

Chapter Two: Two New Friends

Two years later, no one ever went into Midville School and nothing ever came out. The janitor was never found again. Billy had recently moved to town and went to Kilgour Elementary for his new school. He was on his way home when he set foot on the grass of the Midville School property. Not knowing the rumors around town, he walked through the front lawn on the way home from school. He felt a big blast of wind blow him off the property. It felt like a force field. Billy decided to avoid walking that way home again.

He ran into two boys playing catch and asked, "Can I play?"

"Yeah, sure," said one of the boys.

He was tall, had black hair, and had freckles all over his face. The other boy had blond curly hair and was quite short. He introduced himself as John. Billy didn't mention the weird wind—he didn't want to ruin the moment. John tossed the ball to him and to Sam, and for the rest of that afternoon they played catch. Billy was happy to have two new friends.

Chapter Three: The Big Orange

Two weeks later, in math class at Kilgour Elementary, Billy looked out the classroom window to see a crazy, wild banana running toward the school. The banana jumped onto a car parked across the street. Billy was shocked. Bewildered. All the kids were at the window in a matter of seconds.

People were panicking and screaming. Mrs. Wilson, the math teacher, was freaking out. She was frozen in place. They heard pounding above them. Then a giant orange fell through the ceiling. Mrs. Wilson ran out the door screaming. Billy ran over to the window. He yelled for everyone to get out of the classroom, but the orange was in the way.

He jumped on the orange. People behind him fell over. He

jumped up and grabbed the broken ceiling. One hand slipped, but the other barely held on. He looked down. Orange juice was starting to spill out of the orange.

He re-gripped and pulled himself up. His friends, John and Sam, were right behind him. The orange juice had filled the room, and was rising quickly. John, Sam, and Billy helped the others up. Soon, everyone had climbed into the ceiling, except little Rose. Rose was the smallest girl in his grade and she couldn't swim.

The orange juice was now at five feet. Rose was standing on a desk and the juice was up to her chin. Billy jumped down and grabbed her, swam through the orange juice, and stood on the orange to grab the ceiling one more time. Billy pulled Rose up and the class crawled along the ceiling into the next classroom, jumped down, and sprinted down the hall.

Chapter Four: Strawberries and Cherries

The class sprinted down the halls. Other classes started to join them on the way. All the running stopped when they turned a corner to see a strawberry rolling at lightning speed down the hallway. The class turned and sprinted the other way.

The class was two turns away from the front doors when cherries started falling from the ceiling. Kids were getting hit and falling to the ground. Anyone still on their feet pulled them back up. They were a few feet away when a cherry hit Rose in the back. Rose had fallen behind when a cherry knocked her down. No one was nearby to hear her.

The class made it outside, but Billy realized Rose was missing. He took off into the school after her. Sam and John were yelling, but

Billy was only focused on getting to Rose when a cherry slammed into his back. His vision was getting blurry, but out of the corner of his eye he saw the strawberry flying away with Rose. He felt a woozy pain and everything went dark.

Chapter Five: The Rebound

Billy woke up in a hospital bed. He noticed a doctor next to him, looking at a computer. When Billy sat up, the doctor said, "He is awake."

Then he heard two familiar voices—John and Sam.

John and Sam told Billy what had happened. They said after he got knocked down by the cherry, he was trampled by a jumping watermelon. Now they were in the hospital where Sam's mom worked. Then they told Billy the worst part. They thought the fruit monsters might come out of the school.

"It will be risky. Who knows what might be in the school," said Sam.

"We have to do this if we want our town to be the way it was. It could be a life-death situation for all of us if we don't stop them," John replied. "I say tomorrow we go and see what's out there. We will have to tell our parents so they don't get worried."

They agreed that the next day they would check out the school. They gathered all the damaging, threatening weapons they could find in Sam's house. John grabbed a shovel, Sam grabbed an axe, and Billy used a baseball bat. They planned how they would get into the school and what they would do once they got inside. Then, they set off on their journey.

Chapter Six: The Journey to the School

They had been walking for about two blocks when something jumped in their way. It was a grape with long legs and no teeth. The thing grabbed Billy by the shoulders and threw him down on the hard cement. He felt pain surge down his spine.

He saw Sam and John tackling and smacking the thing with their weapons. He tried standing up, but fell. His friends had pinned the grape. Billy felt a stinging pain all over. He felt the boys grabbing his arms and moving him away from the grape. After about five minutes, they stopped and put him on the ground.

The boys sat there for about two minutes in silence, panting, until Sam said, "I think we should get going. We're still about a mile away. You okay, Billy?"

Billy responded, "Yeah, let's keep on going. I'm still worried about running into any more fruits on the way."

They set him in the front yard of an old red house. They took a minute to rest and were back on their feet and Billy started walking on his own. They were only about three blocks away when a giant kiwi fell from the sky onto the mailbox right in front of them. It had skinned Sam's nose and left a big red mark on his nose. The kiwi started to roll toward them. The boys took off the other way, but they had to get around the kiwi if they wanted to make it to the school. So they sprinted for it, past the giant kiwi. With the kiwi on their tail, they made it to the school.

They couldn't find a way in. The kiwi was gaining on them. John spotted the back door open and they ran for it. They made it in, just in time before the kiwi smashed into the wall. They stopped, catching some air.

Chapter Seven: Crazy Mango

They looked at their surroundings. The windows were shattered and the door they had come through had fallen off its hinges. The kiwi still blocked the way out and all of the light. They started walking down the dark, skinny hallway.

Sam broke the silence. "I think we're in the kindergarten hallway. So that means we should go right, if this old, rusty school is still the same."

"I know, but we should hurry before anyone or anything sees us," John said in a worried voice.

The boys were about twenty feet into the hallway when they heard footsteps coming their way. Some boxes were piled in the hallway, and they hid behind them. Two tall bananas with spears walked by.

They tiptoed down the hallway that the bananas came from and came to a broken door on the right. John slowly grabbed the knob and opened it. Something flew through the air and hit Sam hard in the stomach. John and Billy came running over to help. It was a blueberry! More blueberries were coming. One skinned Billy's head. He felt a woozy, sickening feel. He knew they had to get somewhere safe. John and Billy grabbed Sam and they all took off down the hallway. Blueberries were flying. One got John's foot, but they kept moving.

They turned around to see a one-eyed rotten mango with a big bazooka shooting blueberries. One hit John in the face and Billy caught him before he fell. Billy saw a door on the left. He pulled John and Sam through and locked the door. Billy set his friends and his baseball bat down on the floor.

He noticed they were in a janitor closet with mops and cleaning supplies. He heard something rattling in one of the buckets. He slowly walked over, step by step, to see an apple stuck in the bucket. It was small, and was changing colors, from green to yellow to red, like it didn't know which one to choose. Billy took a step back in surprise. He grabbed his bat and held it over the bucket. The thing wasn't there. He turned around and saw the apple inspecting his friends.

Billy slowly and silently walked up behind the apple. He was about to smack the thing away from his friends, when it turned around and just stared at him. He set his bat down. He took another step forward, but the thing scurried under one of the shelves. Billy stood there, waiting. After about a couple minutes or so the thing came out slowly. Billy crept over to it and went into action. He grabbed the thing with both hands.

Chapter Eight: Farla and the Blue Friends

The thing squirmed, trying to get away. "Put me down!"

With a high-pitched squeak, Billy set it down.

Right when it touched the ground, the apple spoke. "You could have put me down a little faster! If you want to cure your friends, then you better scrub them with me."

Billy didn't know what to do. He looked at his friends. They were lying in the corner on some crates and had fallen asleep. They had turned blue. He thought he should probably trust the apple. He grabbed it, dunked it in a bucket of water and, even though it seemed strange, used the apple to scrub his friends. The blue started coming off. Sam and John began to wake up.

When they were clean, Billy put the apple back in the bucket.

The three boys sat there, thinking about what to do. Finally, Sam suggested they go through the gym to the cafeteria and find out what had been going on with the fruit. They grabbed their things and walked out the door, but the apple followed them. They turned around to see it following them. They just looked at it with shock. A few seconds later, the apple spoke. Sam and John were surprised.

She said, "Can I come?"

Billy shrugged his shoulders and said, "Sure."

Sam immediately said, "*No! Are you crazy, Billy? That's an apple.*"

"She's the one who saved you. I scrubbed you guys with her and the blue came off," said Billy.

Sam and John went silent.

"My name is Farla," the apple said.

No one argued when Farla tagged along as they headed toward the cafeteria.

Chapter Nine: The Attack of the Watermelon

They took a left where the crazy mango had been shooting them with blueberries. The mango was nowhere to be seen now. A couple minutes later, they had almost made it to the gym with no harm, but then they were spotted by two watermelon guards. The boys and Farla took off running for the gym, but were cut off by two more watermelon guards.

Farla made the first move. She took off for the biggest watermelon and tackled it. She started munching on the watermelon's leg and it collapsed. That fired all of them up! John took the watermelon on the left and swung his shovel at the thing.

The watermelon responded with a block from his spear. Billy jumped for the watermelon on the right, swinging his bat at the thing. He connected. The watermelon splattered all over the ground. Sam took off toward the last one. He slid right under the watermelon and whacked its back right down the middle. The watermelon split into two.

Sam attacked the watermelon John had missed, swinging his hockey stick and accidentally hitting the wall.

John finally connected. His stick of wood slashed his opponent's feet and chopped them off. Farla ate her watermelon whole, gaining about twenty more pounds. They took off for the gym, only to run into an army of fruit when they got through the door.

Chapter Ten: An Army Defeated with a Miracle

There were blueberries, raspberries, one-eyed pineapples, more ugly mangos, bananas, watermelon guards, even big oranges. It was horrible. It truly was a Fruit Apocalypse!

They snuck around the army of fruit toward the cafeteria door until Farla accidentally slipped on a banana peel. The whole army turned and took off after them.

Two pineapples reached Farla and the boys first. They seemed to be herding them toward the cafeteria door. Just outside, the pineapples stopped and a small blueberry opened the door. Billy, Sam, John, and Farla were pushed through, toward what looked like a throne.

Then, out of nowhere, a humongous pear appeared, sitting on the throne. Billy scanned the cafeteria, looking for something to use as a weapon. His eyes came across something like a cage. He noticed something in it. It was Rose. He remembered what had happened back at Kilgour. The fruits must have captured her and brought her here. He wouldn't mess up this time. He waited for the right moment.

The guards had gone to get the king pear's staff, so Billy made a run for it. He saw the keys on the top of the cage. He jumped and grabbed them, but before he could do anything else, the king pear and his guards had surrounded him.

They had Sam and John. He was screwed. He needed a plan. He couldn't mess this up. Rose had gotten up from her corner and was looking at him. She motioned to the necklace on the king's neck. Billy didn't know what she was trying to tell him, but he decided he should try to break the necklace. He didn't know what else to do.

He put the keys in the lock and the door swung open. He leapt for Sam and John's two capturers and knocked them off their feet. Sam lunged for the pear, but was knocked to the floor. Billy noticed Rose sneaking around the crowd with Farla. He had to get the necklace. Billy lunged at the pear, grabbed his necklace, and yanked it off. The necklace shattered.

The fruits stood frozen with shock, and then they started crumbling into pieces. Billy looked to see Farla crumbling, too. He didn't know what to do. He looked back to see that a human had appeared where King Pear had been.

Sam and John screamed at the same time, "Janitor Jerry!"

Billy didn't know what was going on.

Chapter Eleven: The Truth

The four kids sat down with Janitor Jerry. Janitor Jerry told them what had happened.

"Apparently, the necklace was on the floor in the cafeteria. When I picked it up, light burst out and brought the fruit to life. They wanted to take over the town, but they were trapped in the Midville School with some kind of force field until Billy walked across the front lawn and broke it."

Janitor Jerry walked the kids home and told them how the founder of Kilgour Elementary had found the necklace in his school and didn't know what to do with it, so he gave it to Dave Willsburg, the principal of Midville School.

The other people in town hadn't known what had happened over the past couple days. They'd been inside their homes, hiding, protecting themselves. So, Billy and his friends, along with Rose and Janitor Jerry, were the only ones that knew. The next two weeks were silent and everything was back to normal. The town lived happily ever after, until one day, the vegetables came to town . . .

Billy Sam John

Rose Janitor Jerry

King Pear (Janitor Jerry)

Crazy Mango

Farla

Cherry Bomb

Tall-legged Grape

Watermelon Warrior

Banana Gaurd

rolling Strawberry